Rivalry

JAPANESE STUDIES SERIES

RIVALRY
A Geisha's Tale

Nagai Kafu

TRANSLATED BY STEPHEN SNYDER

Columbia University Press   *New York*

Columbia University Press

Publishers Since 1893

New York   Chichester, West Sussex

Udekurabe © 1917 Nagai Hisamitsu

English translation © 2007 Stephen Snyder

All rights reserved

This book has been selected by the Japanese Literature Publishing Project (JLPP),
which is run by the Japanese Literature Publishing and Promotion Center (J-Lit
Center) on behalf of the Agency for Cultural Affairs of Japan.

Library of Congress Cataloging-in-Publication Data

Nagai, Kafu, 1879–1959.

[Udekurabe. English]

Rivalry : a geisha's tale / Nagai Kafu ; translated from the Japanese
by Stephen Snyder.

p. cm. — (Japanese studies series)

ISBN 978-0-231-14118-5 (cloth : alk. paper)

I. Snyder, Stephen. II. Title. III. Series.

PL812.A4U313   2007

895.6'344—dc22   2007007732

Columbia University Press books are printed
on permanent and durable acid-free paper.

This book is printed on paper with recycled content.

Printed in the United States of America

Designed by Audrey Smith

c 10 9 8 7 6 5 4 3 2 1

Contents

Introduction

Nagai Kafū (1879–1959) began serializing *Rivalry* (*Udekurabe*) in the literary journal *Bunmei* in August 1916, just months after he had resigned his positions as an instructor at Keio gijuku (later Keio University) and as the editor of the influential journal *Mita bungaku*. Just after the turn of the century Kafū was one of the leading figures in a literary movement influenced by French naturalism, but as a member of the antinaturalist school, which included both Mori Ōgai and Natsume Sōseki, he then repudiated that movement. Kafū's sudden retreat from academic and literary life early in 1916 came as something of a surprise, even though it had been prefigured in his work during the years before his resignation. His withdrawal is generally attributed to his well-documented disgust with contemporary Japan, which he saw as a crass and imperfect copy of the modern West, but also to his growing fascination with the past, which for Kafū meant Japan's Edo period (1600–1868). Beginning as early as 1910 and not long after his return from a sojourn in Europe and America, Kafū began writing a series of essays and occasional pieces on various aspects of Edo culture—poetry, theater, *ukiyo-e*, landscape painting—but his real interest lay in the women of the Edo demimonde, the waitresses, courtesans, and geisha whom he saw as the embodiment of the Edo aesthetic and the living repositories of its cultural riches. Accordingly, *Rivalry* can be read as one of the first of Kafū's many literary attempts to discover the traces of this culture in the lives and characters of the women of the Edo pleasure quarters who have survived into the modern age.

The novel is set in the Shimbashi geisha district (*hanamachi*) around 1912. Today Shimbashi is a forest of high-rise apartment towers and postmodern architectural fantasies, but in the early years of the Taishō period (1912–1926) it was home to a large brick train station, the terminus of Japan's first rail line, and the most storied *hanamachi* in Tokyo. A lively commercial center during the Edo period, Shimbashi rose to prominence in the early years of the Meiji period (1868–1912) as the preferred entertainment district of the new political elite. During the Sino-Japanese and Russo-Japanese wars, the quarter solidified its position as the preeminent Tokyo *hanamachi*, with patriotic support for the militarists then in ascendance and elaborate celebrations of the national victories. Like its erstwhile rival Yanagibashi and the lesser quarters as well, this thriving district operated on a complex system of relations among its various inhabitants—geisha, customers, patrons, kabuki actors, and hangers-on—and Kafū's novel excels in depicting these individuals and types as they compete for recognition and supremacy in the quarter. The elaborate pageantry of the novel and the detailed descriptions of the costumes and accoutrements of the geisha and their customers give us a rich sense of the quarter as it must have appeared in this prosperous period when it was a center of national culture and the playground of the wealthy and powerful.

The women of Shimbashi and their business are the central focus of *Rivalry*. Kafū had special reason to be fascinated with the Shimbashi geisha, having been married briefly in 1914 to Yaeji (Uchida Yae), a celebrated dancer in the quarter. The heroine of *Rivalry*, Komayo, who, we may imagine, was partly modeled on

Yaeji, is employed in a geisha house known as the Obanaya, a property owned by Gozan, a practitioner of the traditional storytelling art of *rakugo*, and his wife, Jūkichi, the senior geisha and mistress of the house. The inhabitants include Komayo's fellow geisha, Kikuchiyo and Hanasuke, a *maiko* or dancing girl, an apprentice geisha, maids, and other servants, all of whom are engaged in the business of training and costuming the geisha and sending them off to their nightly round of lucrative engagements. In the system as it existed in the Taishō period, a geisha contracted with a house for lodging, the use of the exorbitantly expensive kimono required for the profession, and the offices of the house in procuring and administering her engagements. These services, along with an initial payment that often went to someone other than the geisha herself, generally meant that she incurred a substantial debt to the house before she began her career. Thus in the early years of the twentieth century, geisha, like the courtesans of the Edo period before them, were often little better than indentured servants in a system that ensured their perpetual dependence on and debt to their house.

The business of the district, however, was transacted not at the geisha houses but at *machiai*, or "teahouses" (the translation of *ochaya*, as these establishments were known in Kyoto), where men, generally men of means, would go to organize parties to which geisha were called from one or more houses. *Machiai* provided rooms where customers, sometimes alone but more often in small groups, would call their preferred geisha for *zashiki* (literally, "drawing room"), a party generally consisting of small talk, drinking, games, and simple entertainment, such as dancing or singing to the accompaniment of a shamisen. The business of the geisha consisted of these nightly parties and the endless practice of their arts (*gei*)—traditional dance, instrumental performance, and singing in traditional ballad styles—that were the pride of their profession and the source of reputations that led to success in the *zashiki*. The story of Komayo's negotiation of the daily demands of her engagements and her rigorous training as a dancer makes up a significant portion of the novel and provides a revealing look at the less glamorous aspects of the geisha's profession.

In *Rivalry*, the men who frequent Shimbashi are typical of the clientele of geisha quarters throughout Japan: politicians, successful businessmen, and artists, as well as various pretenders and buffoons. Kafū sketches a number of these characters—the monstrous antique dealer, the ne'er-do-well writer, the dilettante dramaturge, and the celebrated kabuki actor—and taken together, these portraits constitute a scathing critique of late-Meiji society. For the Western reader, however, the nature of the relations between these men and the geisha in the novel may seem arcane at best. Simply put, for the geisha, customers were essentially divided into two categories: those who called for their services at a *zashiki* on a more or less regular basis, and those who took the next step, attaching themselves to the geisha as a patron, or *danna*. The former paid for the cost of the evening's entertainment, generally in the form of a fee to the *machiai*, a percentage of which was passed along to the geisha and thus to her house. The *danna*, however, made a much more substantial financial commitment, providing a regular stipend to the woman and supporting the costs of musical lessons, artistic performances, and other incidental expenses. The professional goal of the geisha then, and the source of much of the "rivalry" in Kafū's novel, is to procure a wealthy and influential *danna* who might eventually be persuaded to pay off the woman's debt to her house, effectively "ransoming" her, and either marry her in a more or less official sense or set her up in a business of her own. *Rivalry* is perhaps the best depiction of the complex politics and economics of a *hanamachi* in modern Japanese literature, for Kafū is intent on describing not only the lives of the denizens of this milieu but also the dynamics of desire and competition that govern the actions of all the players. As Komayo makes her way through the maze of Shimbashi life, enjoying the successes that her beauty and art bring her but more often suffering the hidden degradations of her profession, a brilliant portrait of an era and a way of life emerges.

A word about the complicated textual history of *Rivalry* and the reasons for a new translation is in order here. After publishing his novel in *Bunmei* from 1916 until October 1917, Kafū made substantial revisions and additions and brought out a private edition of the work late in that year. The additions include the more sexually explicit passages—the first encounter between Komayo and Yoshioka, Komayo's arduous evening in chapter 8, and Kikuchiyo's misadventure in the bath—so Kafū's decision to publish this version privately was based on the knowledge that these passages would be unacceptable to Taishō-era censors. In 1918, a highly expurgated commercial edition appeared, and it was not until 1956 that the material in the private edition was restored in the version that now appears in Iwanami shoten's *Complete Works* and on which this translation is based. I decided to retranslate *Udekurabe* partly because the 1963 translation by Kurt Meissner and Ralph Friedrich is based on the 1918 commercial edition and thus lacks passages, some harrowing and others hilarious, that are vital to our understanding the geisha's experience and Kafū's views of the exploitation and suffering that haunted the lives of women in this profession.

Kafū's novel is among the franker depictions of the sexual component of the geisha's duties. Although much has been written about the overlap or lack of one between the art of the geisha and the business of prostitution, Kafū's account of Komayo's career gives us a clear sense of the dilemma facing the ambitious geisha. The primary business of the geisha of this period may have been entertainment, not prostitution, yet the nature of the patronage system and the economics of attracting and keeping a *danna* meant that most women were effectively engaging in a form of limited prostitution with some if not all their customers. Even though few geisha at the time would have granted sexual favors to a customer at a routine *zashiki*—Kikuchiyo is mentioned as an exception in that regard—there was an expectation of a sexual relationship with the *danna* based on his economic commitment and status as a patron. As Kafū indicates, however, this expectation was sometimes at odds with a woman's feelings, and the depiction of Yoshioka's brutal exercise of his privilege in the third chapter (one of the sections deleted in the expurgated version of the novel) is perhaps Kafū's most direct indictment of gender inequality and the victimization of women in Taishō Japan. *Rivalry* and the portrait of Komayo are among Kafū's most enduring achievements, for their clear-eyed look at the often mysterious world of the geisha and the society that created her.

In the years following the publication of this novel, Kafū continued his withdrawal from literary circles and the fashionable society in which he had moved during the early years of his career. During the 1920s and 1930s and again after World War II, he spent much of his time with the women of the pleasure quarters, first in the popular entertainment district of Asakusa and later in the tawdry new unlicensed quarters east of the Sumida River. As the elegant geisha districts of Shimbashi and Yanagibashi faded, Kafū searched in increasingly obscure and shadowed corners of the city for women who seemed to retain remnants of the Edo spirit. At the beginning of his search, in the pages of *Rivalry*, he left us one of the most memorable portraits of the life and trials and the glamour and degradation of the "world of flower and willow."

Rivalry

1. *Intermission*

It was intermission, and the halls of the Imperial Theater were crowded with people who had left their seats to stretch their legs. A geisha making her way up the main staircase nearly collided with a man on his way down, and their eyes met with a look of startled recognition.

"Yoshioka-san!"

"This is a surprise!"

"It's been years."

"But you're still a geisha?"

"Yes, I'm at it again . . . since the end of last year."

"It's been a while."

"Seven years since I retired."

"Seven years? Has it been that long?"

The bell rang, announcing the start of the next act, and the crush became even worse as people hurried back to their seats. Perhaps thinking no one would notice, the geisha leaned toward him, looking up into his eyes.

"You haven't changed at all," she said.

"Really? And you look even younger than before."

"Don't be ridiculous! At my age . . ."

"No, honestly—not a day older." Yoshioka studied the woman's face with genuine surprise. She would have been seventeen or eighteen when they'd last met. If seven years had passed since then, she must be twenty-five or twenty-six now. But the woman standing before him seemed completely unchanged from the day she had been promoted from apprentice to full-fledged geisha. She was average in height, with large eyes above full, dimpled cheeks. When she smiled, there was something still childlike in the way her eyeteeth came peeking through.

"I hope we can meet again and have a longer chat."

"What name are you using? The same as before?"

"No. I'm Komayo now."

"Komayo? Well then, I'll call for you soon."

"Please do."

The sound of wooden clappers announced the opening of the curtain, and Komayo hurried off down the corridor to the right. Yoshioka started in the opposite direction but then stopped and turned to look back. The lobby was empty except for the girls who worked as ushers and the women from the kiosks who were milling about. Komayo had disappeared. Sitting down on a bench, he lit a cigarette as his thoughts wandered back to what had happened nearly eight years ago. He had graduated at twenty-six and then gone abroad to study for a few years. Returning home, he had found a job, and since then, he was proud to say, he had worked hard for his company. He had dabbled in stocks and acquired some property, and he now had a certain position in society. At the same time, he had also managed to amuse himself, drinking so much over the years that it was surprising his health hadn't suffered. But in all this time, busy as he was with his work and his social life, he had never once had the leisure or the occasion to think back over the past. Tonight, however, after this chance encounter with his first geisha, a woman he had known while he still was at school, for some reason he found himself looking back at that distant time.

As he listened to the strains of the shamisen coming from the stage, the memory of his first outing to Shimbashi brought a smile to his lips. He had been a complete innocent then, and the allure of the geisha world had been irresistible. Nothing in his present life could ever reproduce the sheer delight back then of just being spoken to by one of them. In fact, when he compared himself then with the person he had become today—so used to these pleasures and so calculating in general—he found it made him uncomfortable, even slightly embarrassed. Even his subsequent affairs in the geisha quarter had been arranged almost too carefully; and for the first time he felt as though he were seeing himself clearly as a man who, without quite realizing it, had planned his life down to the last detail. No doubt this was true. It had been less than ten years since he started working for the company, but already he had risen to the position of general manager and was seen as a man of great ability by the president and the board of directors—even if he wasn't very well liked by his colleagues and subordinates.

For about three years now, he had been keeping a geisha named Rikiji who owned a house known as the Minatoya. But he hadn't allowed himself to be deceived the way most patrons were: he knew, because he could see with his own eyes, that she was far from beautiful. She was, however, very good at her art; and no matter where she went, she was immediately recognized as a senior geisha deserving of respect. Yoshioka had long since realized that it would be useful for his professional life to have the ready services of a geisha or two for banquets and business parties; and with an eye to avoiding unnecessary expenditures, he had recruited Rikiji by convincing her that he was in love with her.

At the same time, he kept another woman as his mistress. She was the proprietress of the Murasaki *machiai*, a house of assignation in Hama-chō that suited the standards of that district. She had once been a waitress in a restaurant in Daichi, and like so many men who grow tired of courting geisha only to find themselves in worse trouble than before, he had tumbled into bed with her one night when he was drunk. He regretted it almost immediately, worrying about what the geisha he knew would say if they found out he had taken up with a waitress. But this had been the woman's strategy from the beginning, and he had agreed to provide the funds to open the Murasaki in exchange for her promise to keep their affair a secret and cause him no more difficulties. Fortunately, the Murasaki turned out to be a success, and its rooms were full every evening. When Yoshioka saw how things were going, he realized that he would be a fool to stay away from a place in which he already had a considerable investment. So he dropped in once or twice for a drink, and soon he had quietly renewed his affair with the proprietress. A large woman with pale, ample flesh, she was turning thirty this year. She was, of course, more sophisticated than a true amateur, but when compared with a geisha, she clearly lacked a certain quality and seemed a bit plodding and heavy. In other words, it was not affection that led him back to her whenever he'd had a bit to drink, but sexual appetite, stirred by that energetic manner peculiar to serving girls of the pleasure quarters. Even though he immediately regretted each meeting, his regrets did not stop him from going back again and again, and it became clear that their relationship was as inescapable as it was unfortunate.

Compared with such complicated matters, when Yoshioka looked back on the simple, innocent affection he'd had for Komayo—she was just eighteen and he twenty-five when they first had become intimate—he had the agreeable feeling that he was watching a play or perhaps reading a novel. It was all so delightful that it seemed quite unreal.

At this moment, a short, stout man in a suit came up to Yoshioka. "Oh, there you are. I've been looking everywhere for you." The man apparently had drunk a good deal—most likely in the dining room on the second floor of the theater—and his round face was bright red, his nose beaded with sweat. "There was a phone call for you."

"From where?"

"The same place as usual." After checking to make sure they were alone, the fat little man sat down next to Yoshioka. "It seems that lately you haven't been stopping in at the Minatoya very often."

"Did she call you to the phone?"

"She did. I wondered who it could be, and I was even a bit flattered. But as usual, it was for you. I couldn't help feeling a little sorry for myself." The man burst out laughing.

"Then she knows we're here tonight."

"Someone must have told her. At any rate, she said you should stop by on your way home, even if it's just for a minute."

"No, Eda, my friend, the fact is I've got something more entertaining in mind for tonight." Yoshioka offered him a gold-tipped cigarette as he glanced around the room. "Let's go to the restaurant."

"Something to do with that affair in Hama-chō?"

"No, not that old story. This is a romance."

"A romance?"

"It's like something out of a novel."

"A novel? Don't keep me in suspense," he said as he followed Yoshioka through the lobby to the spacious restaurant downstairs.

"Whiskey as usual?"

"No, I've had a good bit already tonight. I'll stick to beer. It's a bit early to let myself go." He laughed again, and his whole body shook as he mopped his wrinkled forehead with his handkerchief. Anyone watching them would have understood immediately from his appearance and his manner that he was little more than Yoshioka's sidekick. Although they seemed to be about the same age, Eda's curly hair was thinning to the point that he was half bald. His duties involved handling the stock in the firm at which Yoshioka was a manager; but since he was always arranging company banquets and parties, he was as well known in the pleasure quarters as Yoshioka was, despite the difference in their positions. Any geisha you might ask, and even the maids at the teahouses, would tell you that Eda was a funny, harmless little man with a fondness for saké; and even when familiarity led, from time to time, to such unflattering comments slipping out in his presence, he never took offense. On the contrary, the more they made fun of him, the better he seemed to like it, and he often would join in, agreeing that he was no use to anyone. To hear him, nobody would have imagined that he had three children at home, the eldest a daughter who would soon be reaching marriageable age.

"But what's so 'entertaining'?" he asked, picking up the beer that the waiter had left in front of him. "Don't tell me that you've launched into a new adventure without warning me, your faithful retainer." He could barely contain his curiosity.

"In fact, that's exactly what I'm hoping."

"You're up to your old tricks then!"

"Eda, be serious. I think I may have fallen in love tonight for the first time in my life." Yoshioka looked around to see whether anyone was nearby, but the large room was empty except for a few waiters huddled together in a distant corner. The lamps shining on the white tablecloths set off the brilliant colors of the flowers arranged in the Western style.

"I'm serious about this," Yoshioka said.

"I can see that. And I'm all ears."

"But everything's a joke to you. Which is why it's so hard to tell you anything. The truth is, I met her just now, quite by accident, on the staircase."

"And . . . ?"

"She's someone I knew when I was still in school."

"A proper young lady? And let me guess, she's married now."

"You're getting ahead of yourself. She's a geisha."

"A geisha? Then you must have begun your 'training' at a tender age."

"She was the first geisha I met, when I was just starting out. She was known as Komazō back then. It lasted about a year, until I graduated and went abroad. But we parted on good terms."

"I see," said Eda, puffing away at the cigarette Yoshioka had given him.

"It seems she's come back to Shimbashi after seven years away, and she's calling herself Komayo now."

"Komayo? . . . From which house?"

"I didn't get anything but her name. I don't know whether she has her own place or works for a house."

"A few discreet inquires, and we'll soon find out."

"At any rate, there must be some reason she's become a geisha again after giving it up for seven years. I'd love to know more about her and who was looking after her all that time."

"So you want a thorough investigation."

"I don't see any other option. When you're getting into something like this, it's always best to know everything right from the start. How many poor fools have made an enemy by seducing a friend's woman without realizing it?"

"Well, if things are really moving along that quickly, we should get busy. I'll need to have a look at her, at the very least. Where's she sitting? In a box?"

"I met her in the lobby. I don't know where she is."

"Well then, I take it you're planning to stop somewhere on your way home? I'll go with you and you can call her in. Then I'll be able to offer you an expert opinion."

"That sounds like a good idea."

"So Rikiji is finally going to be a woman scorned. The poor thing!" Eda was laughing again.

"That's hardly my problem. You of all people know how much I've done for her. She'll be fine without me. She has four or five geisha under contract and a string of regular customers."

Yoshioka cut the conversation short as people began wandering in from the corridor, talking in loud voices. From the stage, they could hear the echo of the wooden clappers signaling a battle scene.

"Waiter!" Yoshioka called, rising from his chair. "The check!"

2. A Real Gem

"Welcome," said the mistress of the Hamazaki teahouse, kneeling respectfully in the anteroom. "And where have you spent the evening?"

"We were invited to the Imperial. Fujita-san wanted us to see a play in the new style, one with women in the cast." Yoshioka stood in the main room, preoccupied with removing the *hakama* trousers he wore over his kimono. "It's no easy matter, being the patron of an actress. You always have to provide her with an audience."

"I suppose so. It's much simpler with geisha," said the mistress, taking her place next to a table made of rosewood. "Eda-san, you must be terribly warm. Wouldn't you like to change into something more comfortable?"

"I am a bit warm, but I don't think I will tonight. I don't like wearing a *yukata*—it makes me look like that character in *Iseondo* who gets cut to ribbons."

"But there's no need to be so formal."

"Actually, there is something we'd like you to do for us."

"Of course."

"I'd like to play host tonight. And I want you to call in some different geisha from the usual ones."

"Very well. But who did you have in mind?"

"Well, to begin with, we won't be calling Rikiji."

"Really? But why not?"

"I told you that we have a favor to ask. You'll understand soon enough."

"But still . . ." She looked dubiously in Yoshioka's direction, but he just smiled and puffed away at his cigar. A maid brought in saké and appetizers. Eda quickly drained his cup and held it out to the mistress.

"Could you get the one named Komayo? That's 'Ko-ma-yo.'"

"Komayo . . . ," the mistress repeated, turning to look at the maid.

"She's a new girl. Quite beautiful," Eda prompted.

"Oh, she's from Ju-san's house," the maid said, as if just remembering.

"From Ju-san's?" said the mistress, seeming to have understood at last. She set her cup on the table. "She hasn't been here yet, has she?"

"No, she has," the maid replied. "She stopped by to pay her respects the day before yesterday at the party served by Chiyo-matsu-san."

"Yes, now I remember. The one with the small, round face. The older I get, the harder it is to tell one from the other."

"And who else?" Eda said, turning to Yoshioka. "We haven't had Jūkichi in some time. It might be best to have another woman from the same house."

"That's fine with me."

"Very well," said the maid, before collecting the teapot and cups on her tray and leaving the room.

"But I'm afraid I don't understand any of this," said the mistress, returning the saké cup to Eda.

"There's no reason you should," Eda laughed. "It's all come up suddenly, just this evening. To tell the truth, I'm confused myself." He laughed again. "At any rate, I'm dying to see if she'll come."

"And I'm still in the dark."

"Well, just sit back and relax. It promises to be quite interesting. . . ."

The maid returned. "They said that Komayo-san is at the theater. She should be along shortly."

At this, Eda burst out laughing, to the mistress's consternation.

"Forgive me," said Eda, regaining his composure. "And what about the others?"

"Jūkichi and the others won't be able to come for a while. What would you like me to do?"

"Well . . . ," said Eda, looking over at Yoshioka, "tell them to come when they can." This time, the mistress herself rose to go to the phone, leaving the maid with them. "All the better," Eda continued. "If she's by herself, things are likely to move along more quickly."

"O-Chō," said Yoshioka, holding out a cup for the maid. "Join us for a drink. And tell me, do you know if Komayo has a patron?"

"She's a fine geisha, isn't she?" said the maid, ignoring the question. "They say she's worked in the quarter before." Eda's laughter filled the room again. "You seem to find everything amusing this evening, Eda-san."

"I can't help it. It *is* amusing. Didn't you know? Komayo is my geisha, or she was, seven years ago. When I first began coming here, the girls made quite a fuss over me."

"Really?! Over you?" Now the maid was laughing.

"Is that so funny? You don't need to be rude."

"It's true," said Yoshioka. "I'm a witness. She was quite wild about him for a time, but then it ended. They're meeting again tonight for the first time in ten years."

"Well, if it's true, it's quite a story."

"What do you mean, 'if it's true'? Don't be so suspicious, O-Chō. I was much thinner back then, and I had all my hair. You should have seen me." Eda went on talking until at last they heard footsteps in the corridor.

"Is this the room?" said a young woman's voice.

Eda pulled himself up into a more proper posture. The door slid open. It was Komayo.

Her hair was done in a low *shimada* style with an openwork, silver-covered comb and a jade hairpin. She had changed into a kimono of light crepe with a fine stripe. The effect was quite refined, but perhaps fearing it would seem too old for her, she had added a half collar with elaborate embroidery. Her obi was made of crepe in the old-fashioned Kaga style, lined with black satin, and it was held together with a sash of light blue crepe dyed in a bold pattern. The cord worn over the obi was a deep celadon green decorated in front with a large pearl.

"What a surprise, running into you . . . ," she said, greeting Yoshioka. But then, noticing Eda's unfamiliar face, she started again in a slightly different tone. "Good evening."

Eda lost no time in offering her a cup. "Have you come from the theater?"

"Yes. Were you there as well?"

"We had planned to invite you here as we were leaving, but we didn't know where you were sitting." As he spoke, Eda discreetly took stock of Komayo's costume, her accessories, and her way of conducting herself in front of guests. None of this, of course, concerned him directly. But since he was in the habit of amusing himself in the company of such women without partaking of the erotic possibilities, he was determined this evening, for Yoshioka's sake, to make an accurate assessment of Komayo's worth as a geisha through the eyes of an impartial observer. Every woman in the quarter bore the title of "Shimbashi geisha," but he knew that they represented a wide range of quality and that it would never do for Yoshioka to take up with one of the more common sort, regardless of some previous attachment between them. There was a difference between the Yoshioka of his student days and the man of affairs he had become today, and Eda realized that for tonight at least, he would have to forgo his usual drinking in order to play the role of mother hen.

For Yoshioka, the principal in the affair, the matter was even more delicate. Was Komayo tied by a debt somewhere or perhaps under contract to a geisha house? Or was she just working to amuse herself? There was no need to be rude and ask such things straight out. He would study her manner, the way she dressed, and drawing on his intimate knowledge of geisha, he would reach his own conclusions.

Komayo carefully rinsed the saké cup, returned it to Eda, and then gracefully refilled it. She couldn't be sure, but based on her experiences in the quarter, she was fairly confident that she could guess the relationship between the two men, even though she was meeting Eda for the first time tonight. Still, out of prudence, she limited herself to small talk.

"It's already too hot for the theater, don't you think?"

"Komayo," said Yoshioka, his tone abrupt but quite familiar. "How old are you now?"

"My age? Do we have to talk about that? But what about you, Yoshioka-san?"

"I'm already forty."

"You can't be serious!" she said. Cocking her head to one side like a little girl, she began counting on her fingers and murmuring to herself. "I was seventeen then . . . and it's been how many years now . . . ?"

"You'd best be careful," said Eda, interrupting her. "We're all ears."

"I'm sorry. It's just that . . ."

"'Then,' 'now'—when, exactly, are we talking about?"

Komayo began to laugh, revealing her pretty teeth. "Yoshioka-san, you can't be more than thirty-five or so."

"Do you mind if we talk about more personal matters?" said Yoshioka.

"About you?"

"No, about you. After I left to go abroad, how long did you work as a geisha?"

"Let me see," said Komayo. She glanced up at the ceiling for a moment as she played with her fan. "It was two more years before I quit."

"Then it would have been just about the time I got back from overseas." He would have liked to ask her who had taken her away from the quarter, but he couldn't bring himself to do so. "So you prefer being a geisha to the life of an honest woman?" he said, trying to make the question sound casual.

"I didn't necessarily want to come back," she said. "But there wasn't anything else for me to do."

"Were you someone's mistress, or were you actually married?"

Komayo slowly emptied her cup and then set it on the table. She was silent for a moment but then seemed to make up her mind. "There's really no point in hiding anything," she said, shifting slightly closer. "I was properly married for a while. It was after you left and everything ended. I have to admit that I was quite miserable just then." She laughed. "It's true! But about the same time I happened to meet a young man from a rich country family who had come to Tokyo to study. He offered to pay off my debt to the house."

"How lucky for you."

"For a while I was his mistress, but then he wanted me to go home to the country with him. He said he would marry me if I did. I didn't really like the idea, but I realized I wouldn't be young forever and marriage seemed like a good idea—or at least it did at the time."

"And where was his home?"

"Ever so far away. The place where they catch all the salmon."

"Niigata?"

"No, not there. Up toward Hokkaido. You know . . . Akita. It's terribly cold there. I'll never forget it. Three long years I put up with that place."

"And finally you couldn't stand it any more?"

"Why do you say that? No, my husband died. And to his family, I was still a geisha at heart. His parents were important people, and there were two younger brothers. Under the circumstances, I really couldn't stay on there by myself."

"No, I suppose you couldn't. . . . Well, why don't you relax now and have another drink?"

"Thank you," Komayo said, taking the cup that Eda had filled. "Now you know what happened, and I hope I can count on your kindness."

"I wonder what's become of the other girls. I doubt they'll be coming now."

"It's not eleven yet," Eda said, taking out his watch. At that moment Komayo was called to the telephone. As he watched her go, Eda lowered his voice. "She's quite a woman, isn't she? A real gem."

Yoshioka laughed.

"It's just as well that none of the others came. And I should be going, too."

"Don't be silly. Things haven't reached that point yet, and this isn't a one-night affair."

"But you've gone too far to turn back now, and she's probably feeling the same way. You wouldn't want to embarrass her." In one motion, Eda emptied the two saké cups that were in front of him. Then, helping himself to a cigar from Yoshioka's tobacco case, he struck a match and got to his feet.

3. Dayflowers

After answering a call from the attendant at her geisha house, Komayo was about to rejoin her guests when the mistress called to her from behind the counter.

"Koma-chan, do you have a moment?"

"Okami-san, do you suppose I could leave now?" Komayo said, in the hope of deflecting the woman's questions.

"You'll have to go ask them," the mistress said. She was used to situations like this. "Anyway, he never stays the night," she added, blowing a puff of smoke. Her tone implied that everything was already settled.

Komayo was suddenly at a loss for an answer. Yoshioka-san was, of course, a client from her earlier career, so she could hardly make objections now. And indeed, she found him quite agreeable.

Still, for things to end up like this on the first night, when he had called for her after such a long time—she feared that the teahouse world would think badly of her and see her as exactly the sort of kept geisha she had been in her youth. Furthermore, she didn't know yet what Yoshioka-san was thinking. But he'd been on his way home after running into her at the theater, and she wouldn't be surprised if he had called her with that in mind; after all, it would hardly be their first encounter. Still, if that were the case, he could have made his intentions clear with a wink or some other signal, without going through the teahouse. That would have been so much better for her reputation, she thought, mildly annoyed.

"Well then, please let me know when I can go," she said, and without waiting for an answer she went back to the room on the second floor. The light revealed the clutter of discarded cups and plates on the rosewood table, but there was no sign of either Yoshioka or Eda. She realized they had probably just gone to the bathroom, but she was suddenly overcome with an inexplicable sense of abandonment. As if trying to ward off the feeling, she settled down under the lamp and, from force of habit, reached for the small mirror she kept tucked in her sash. She smoothed her hair and wiped her face with a powdered tissue; and as she stared absentmindedly at the mirror, she was overtaken by the worries that continually seemed to afflict her.

As far as she was concerned, they were not about her love life. But in fact, her love life could indeed be said to be the source of her troubles, even though Komayo herself refused to believe that her difficulties stemmed from anything so frivolous. In her mind, her sole concern was her future. She was twenty-six this year, and her youth would not last forever. If she didn't make plans soon, there would be nothing but vexation and helplessness to look forward to. She had been apprenticed at fourteen, and at sixteen she had begun serving saké at banquets. When she was nearly twenty, her debt to the house had been paid, and when she was twenty-two her patron had taken her to his home in Akita; but she had lost him three years later. Until the day he died, she had known nothing of the world or of human nature, and she never had given any real thought to what would become of her. If she had wanted to stay on in Akita, she probably could have done so, but she would have been resigning herself to an existence that would have been plainer than a nun's. She had been left utterly alone with this well-to-do country family, with people who were completely different from her in every way; and she knew that it was not a place where a city-bred girl would be able to live out her life. For a time, she had considered doing away with herself, but at last she had fled to Tokyo without any clear idea of what she would do there.

When she arrived at Ueno Station, however, she realized that she had no place to go. It had been many years since she had had contact with her own family, and other than the geisha house in Shimbashi that had originally purchased her contract, there was nowhere in all of Tokyo that would take her in. Now, for the first time in her life, Komayo began to fully understand the hardship and sadness of being a woman on her own. At the same time she was painfully aware that whatever happened, she would have to make her own way in the world. If she went to the house where she was first apprenticed, she was sure she would find a place to stay for the time being as well as some sort of help with her future. But in a moment of feminine pique, she realized that it would be too painful to return to a place from which she'd been ransomed so handsomely seven years earlier. After she had already boarded the train for Shimbashi, she decided she would rather die than go there. But suddenly a voice broke in on her thoughts, calling her by the name she had used in the old days: Komazō. Startled, she looked around. It was O-Ryū, the maid at the teahouse that her husband from Akita had favored. It seemed that after many years of patient service, she had succeeded in opening her own establishment in the southern part of the quarter, and after much urging, Komayo gratefully accepted her offer of lodging. Soon after that, she had become attached to her present house, the Obanaya, which was run by an old geisha named Jūkichi. They had agreed on an arrangement in which Komayo would share her profits with the house.

The voice of a young geisha interrupted these reflections.

"No, stop . . . please!" There was laughter from several hoarse voices. Komayo looked around the room in surprise. "No, not again. You really are horrible."

There was more laughter from the men, and the woman herself began to giggle. The sounds were coming from the second floor of the neighboring teahouse, separated from their own by a tiny garden no larger than a few square yards.

It suddenly occurred to Komayo how much she hated being a geisha. Once you had entered this life, they could do what they wanted with you. She'd been a married woman in a fine family, respected by all the servants—the thought left her on the verge of tears.

Just then, a maid came hurrying down the corridor. "Komayo-san!" she cried. "Where have you been?" She began clearing away the cups and dishes. "He's over there, in the annex."

"All right," Komayo said. She felt her heart skip a beat and her face grow flushed, but she got quietly to her feet, gathered up the hem of her kimono, and went down the stairs. As she was doing so, however, her mood suddenly changed. The depression she had been feeling melted away, and she concluded that if she were going to make a success of herself, it would do no good to go about things halfheartedly. Like a good businesswoman, she was determined to find her client and make sure the seeds that had been planted came to fruit. Passing along the veranda that encircled the building, she opened the cedarwood door at the end. She found a wood-floored vestibule that was pitch dark and, beyond that, an antechamber of just three tatami mats. The sliding doors into the main room were standing wide open, but the panels of the folding screen that had been set up in the room obstructed the view beyond. The ceiling was covered with wickerwork, through which the cord of the electric lamp hung down. Its light illuminated the cigar smoke that was rising from behind the screen.

Komayo suddenly felt as though she had been transported back seven years to the days when she was under the complete control of her geisha house. This time, although she had been working as a geisha again for nearly six months, she had kept herself aloof without really seeming to and had managed politely to escape every proposal she encountered at the teahouses. In fact, until tonight, she had not found herself in a room fitted out with the fateful screen.

She had thought she would call to Yoshioka from this ante-chamber, but then she froze, realizing that her entrance had been too quiet. Fortunately, as she stood hesitating, he sensed that someone was behind the screen.

"Is that you, O-Chō?" He was calling the maid, but Komayo seized the opportunity.

"Let me help you," she said, folding back one side of the screen.

Yoshioka had already changed into a *yukata* and was sitting cross-legged on the futon smoking a cigar. He turned toward her.

"Oh, it's you," he said, grinning.

Komayo felt her heart leap again and her face redden. She lowered her eyes without answering.

"Are you all right? It's been a long time," he said, placing his hand lightly on her shoulder.

"It feels strange," she said, covering her embarrassment by feeling in her sleeve for the small bag that held her cigarette case. "It was all so long ago that now it seems funny somehow."

Yoshioka's gaze moved slowly from her neck to her profile, and his voice grew softer.

"Komayo, would you like to stay here tonight?"

She did not answer, but bringing the knot in the cord of her tobacco pouch to her mouth to try to loosen it, she tilted her head toward him and smiled.

"Wouldn't that be difficult for you?"

"Not at all. But I'm afraid I won't be able to live up to my wild student days. Those were good times, weren't they?" He gave her hand a squeeze.

"They were. We had our fun. . . . But what would happen if we carried on like that now?" she said, finally lighting her cigarette. She glanced at Yoshioka again. "At the very least, your wife would hate me."

"My wife? She gave up worrying about me long ago. She wouldn't even notice."

"Then the other geisha . . . ," Komayo said, lying back now on the futon, apparently having overcome her embarrassment. "But I suppose it hardly matters. And if someone did say something, I'd be ready."

"Meaning what?"

"That I've known you longer than anyone else. Isn't that right?"

"It's true! More than ten years." Yoshioka laughed.

"I've got a slight headache this evening," Komayo said. "The theater was suffocating. . . ." As she began at last to undo the sash that held together her obi, she cried out in frustration.

"What is it?"

"I can't get it undone. It's tied too tightly. Look, my fingers are all red." She held up her hands for him to see. "I like it tight, though. If it's not so tight that it takes your breath away, it just doesn't feel right."

She dropped her chin to her chest and worked away at the knot, but it was quite stubborn.

"Here, let me see," said Yoshioka, crawling out from under the quilt.

"It won't budge," she said. Abandoning the project to Yoshioka, she began to remove all the items she had tucked into the obi: her purse, a notepad, a small mirror, a toothpick holder.

"It is tight," Yoshioka said. "And it can't be good for your health."

"There, we've got it now. I'm sorry." Komayo took a deep breath and got to her feet. The ornament on her sash fell to the floor and, moving over to stand by the wall, she turned away and began to untie the obi.

Puffing on his cigar, Yoshioka gazed at Komayo as she un-wrapped the long, scarlet *habutae*-silk undersash that was tied around her waist. The material fell in swirls on the hem of her loosened kimono. Seven years earlier, when she had been barely twenty years old, she already had shown a woman's knowledge of how to behave in such circumstances. Now, accustomed though Yoshioka was to worldly pleasures, he found himself throbbing with impatience and curiosity as she unwound the seemingly endless sash. How had she changed? How would she look now that she was in her twenties, had suffered to a certain degree, and had become a real woman? The feeling was more acute than it would have been had he been meeting her for the first time.

Finished at last unwinding the sash, she turned to face him. As she did so, the weight of her heavy kimono caused it to slip down over her rounded shoulders, leaving her standing under the light in a single underkimono. This light summer robe of white crepe was covered in a design of dayflowers by a stream, the flowers dyed a deep indigo with pale green foliage dotted with delicate dewdrops. In this part of Tokyo, the material could have come only from the Erien, which prided itself on such luxu-rious products. Under normal circumstances, Yoshioka might have made some comment about the robe, but now he had no time for such niceties, impatient as he was to have her in his arms. Apparently oblivious to his feelings, Komayo remained standing where she was. She used her foot to gently push away the discarded kimono and then seemed to discover the cotton robe that had been laid out for her.

"Ah, they've left a *yukata*," she murmured to herself as if seized by some perverse feminine desire to avoid soiling her silk underkimono with perspiration. At the prospect of still more de-lays, Yoshioka began to seem slightly exasperated.

"I'm sure you're fine like that," he said. But she was already busy undoing the end of the undersash of Hakata cloth. Sliding both the silk dayflower robe and her underlayer from her shoulders, she stood facing him, the white skin of her naked body shining like snow in the lamplight. As she stooped to pick up the *yukata*, Yoshioka could no longer control himself and grabbed her hand, pulling her to him.

"What are you doing?" she cried, stumbling forward in spite of herself. He was just in time to catch her firm, plump body as she fell toward him, and then as she struggled halfheartedly, he whispered in her ear.

"Komayo. It's been seven years."

"I'd die if you left me again," she sighed. Then knowing what was in store, she quickly closed her eyes to hide her discomfort.

They said nothing more. The man's face grew bright red as if he were drunk, and the veins in his arms and neck stood out. For her part, Komayo lay as if dead, her head resting on his arm while her hair, done up in the gingko-leaf style, fell loose. As the heart beneath her naked breasts began to beat more quickly, her clenched lips parted, and from between her pretty teeth the tip of her tongue appeared.

Bringing his face close to hers, he gently placed his mouth against her lips. He held her there, ignoring the pain in the arm that was supporting her head; but eventually he began to move his lips over her body, choosing, one after the other, even softer, silkier spots—the tip of her breast, her earlobe, an eyelid, a place under her chin.

Her breath quickened each time he moved, and he could feel it hot on his shoulder. Soon Komayo began to cry out as if in pain, and without quite realizing it, she pushed out the leg that had been folded under her. As she turned to meet him, her arms, which had been lying limp on the tatami, reached out to encircle his body. Her breath became ragged and hot, and she moaned again as her arms squeezed him with alarming force.

The comb fell from her hair, and at the sound her eyes came half open. "Darling, turn out the lights. Please," she said in a faltering voice as if she'd just realized that the room was brightly lit. But her words were interrupted by another kiss. Soon she was worried less about concealing herself than with her increasingly frantic breathing, which sounded only as if she were urging him on. Yoshioka let her slip gently from his arms onto the futon and pulled up the linen coverlet, but he had no intention of putting out the light. He wanted to see every detail of her expression, every inch of her body as she writhed with pleasure. He wanted to see her beg him to stop. Among all his experiences, this was the richest; among all the postures and poses he had seen in erotic prints, these were the most exotic—and he wanted to study them with his eyes wide open.

4. *Welcoming Fires*

The market selling decorations for the O-Bon festival, which had kept the Ginza filled with shoppers far into the night, had ended yesterday. This evening, the side streets lined with geisha houses were alive with shouts of "O-mukai, o-mukai" from vendors selling materials for the fires to welcome the souls of the dead, and boys poured from the newspaper office on the main street calling "Extra! Extra!" and ringing their bells as if something important had happened. Here and there, geisha could be seen hurrying off to their engagements in *rikisha* while the sound of steel struck on flint—a good luck custom—could be heard from the lattice doors of their houses. Over the hustle and bustle of the summer night in the city, the crescent moon and the evening star shone with a cool, brilliant light.

The door of the Obanaya rattled open, and an old man emerged. "A special edition? Probably another airplane crash."

As he studied the sky with a quizzical look, he heard the

charming voice of an apprentice geisha behind him. "*Danna*, are you going to light the welcome fire now?"

"I suppose so," he said. He stood with his hands behind his back still looking up at the sky and continued as if to himself: "This year we'll have a new moon for O-Bon."

"*Danna*, what does it mean to have a new moon for O-Bon?" Hanako made a clicking sound with the rubber toy she held in her mouth. The old man's soliloquy must have sounded odd to the young apprentice.

"The things I bought for the fire are under the family altar. Would you bring them out?"

"Could I light it?"

"Yes, but go get them now, and be careful not to break the brazier."

"Of course," she called, barely able to contain her excitement at the chance to light the fire. She was back in a moment, bringing the wood to the edge of the street.

"It's ready. I'll light it now."

"Take your time. It's dangerous to burn it all at once." Even as he spoke, the fire flared up in the evening breeze blowing from the main street, its light dyeing the girl's heavily powdered face a deep crimson. The old man crouched down and joined his palms to pray. "Namu Amida Butsu. Namu Amida Butsu."

"Look! They've lit fires at Chiyokichi's and across the way! How beautiful!" Somehow out of place in the new city of telephones and electric lights, the smoke from the fires gave the quarter a melancholy air. The old man of the Obanaya continued his prayers for a long while, but at last he stood up, rubbing his hips with both hands. He had long since passed the age of sixty. His hempen summer kimono, worn thin with endless washings, was tied with a black satin sash that appeared to be made from a woman's obi. His body was not yet noticeably bent with age, but his arms and legs were very thin, as if he were so much skin and bones. Although his head was completely bald, his cheeks sunken, and his snow white eyebrows as long as the bristles of a brush, he seemed to be a contented old man. For someone of his age, his eyes were bright and his jaw firm. His nose had an elegant line, and to look at him one would never have thought he had spent his life as the master of a geisha house.

"Oh, *danna*! The sensei from Negishi is coming."

"Where?" The old man had been sprinkling water on the embers of the fire, but he looked up now. "So he is. You young people have such sharp eyes."

Catching sight of the old man from several houses away, the man whom Hanako called the Negishi sensei, put his hand to his hat and uttered a loud "Hello!" It was, in fact, Kurayama Nansō, a writer of novels for serialization, and he was making his way toward them, taking large strides to avoid the puddles in the street. Aged about forty, he wore a jacket of fine, plain silk over a white summer kimono, and on his feet were snow white socks and leather-soled sandals. His appearance did not suggest an office worker or a shopkeeper, nor did he look much like an actor. For some years now he had been diligently turning out serial novels for the Tokyo newspapers, and from time to time he would write a play for the kabuki stage. He also wrote *jōruri* ballads and theater reviews, and from the sum of these activities he had made something of a name for himself.

"Please come in," the old man said, sliding open the lattice door. But the novelist stood for a moment, watching as the smoke from the O-Bon fires drifted through the alley.

"It's only during O-Bon and the equinox festivals that I seem to be able to recapture the feeling of the past. Which reminds me, your son Shō. . . . How many years is it now?"

"Shōhachi? It's been six years."

"Six years already? So next year will be the seventh anniversary."

"Yes, that's right," said the old man. "Death comes to us all, old and young, but there's nothing harder to understand than the uncertainty of life."

"They seem to be having lots of memorial performances at the theaters this year. Are you planning something for the anniversary? Hasn't someone mentioned it?"

"They have, actually. In fact, we talked about doing something for the third anniversary, but it seemed like too much fuss to make for a boy, so we let it drop."

"I don't agree. He was a fine actor and his loss was a terrible blow."

"If he had lived a few more years, we would have seen what became of him, but he was just a beginner. No matter how talented you are, if you die at twenty-three or twenty-four, you're still little more than an apprentice. The only ones who really feel the loss are his family and maybe a few others who were drawn to him. So a grand memorial performance for the third or seventh anniversary, as if he had been one of the great actors of his time—well, it would only be tempting fate."

"I understand why you feel that way. But if the idea came from his former patrons, then it wouldn't be as if you had brought it up or were inconveniencing anyone. Why not leave it to someone else?"

"I'm sure you're right. I'll let them handle it the way they want. It's probably better for an old man to keep quiet."

So saying, he led the writer to a small room at the back of the house. For the modest Obanaya, it was the best room, but since it was also where the old man and his wife, Jūkichi, a senior geisha, had lived for many years, the family's Buddhist altar occupied one corner. A little garden, just a few yards square but decorated with a lighted stone lantern, lay between it and a slightly larger room where the geisha came and went. Beyond that, the lattice door and window that opened onto the street were visible through the reed screen of the veranda. The cool evening breeze blew through the narrow passage that separated the Obanaya from the house next door, ringing the wind chime that hung from the eaves.

"As usual, the room is a mess," the old man said. "But please take off your jacket."

"No thank you. I'm quite comfortable. There's a wonderful

breeze." Fluttering his fan, Kurayama had just begun to look around the room with apparent interest when a geisha entered carrying a tobacco tray and a dish of cakes. It was Komayo. She had already encountered Kurayama at the Obanaya on two or three previous occasions, but she also knew him from a number of banquets and teahouse parties, as well as plays and performances where their paths had crossed. So her tone was familiar when she greeted him.

"Sensei, it's nice to see you."

"It's nice to see you, too. I've been wanting to tell you how much I enjoyed your splendid performance the other day. I feel as though you should be offering me some sort of treat to celebrate."

"Really? What an idea! What kind of treat could someone like me offer you?"

"Well, I'm sure I could suggest something if you wouldn't mind my speaking in front of the master here." Kurayama laughed.

"By all means, if you have something to say, say it. I have nothing to feel guilty about." Komayo laughed brightly as she stood up. Just at that moment, Hanako, the apprentice, called shrilly from the front of the house.

"Komayo! You have an engagement."

"All right!" she answered. "Sensei," she said, turning to Kurayama, "you must excuse me." Then she quietly left the room.

Kurayama tapped his cigarette on the ashtray. "It's always lively around here, isn't it?" he said. "How many girls do you have?"

"At the moment, three grown and two young ones. It keeps us busy."

"This must be just about the oldest house in Shimbashi. When was it started?"

"Well, let's see. I'll never forget the first time I came to Shimbashi for a bit of fun. It was at the height of the Satsuma Rebellion. Jūkichi's mother was still healthy in those days—the two of them did quite well for themselves. The world's changed since then. In those days, Shimbashi was an elegant neighborhood, like the Yamanote is now. Back then, Yanagibashi was the best place for geisha, and going on down the line, there was Sanya-bori, Yoshichō, and Sukiyamachi in Shitaya. Until quite recently, in places like Akasaka, the geisha would come to parties even if they were held in the rooms above noodle shops; they would do just about anything you wanted for a twenty-sen tip. You can imagine how people came running, just for the novelty of it."

While Kurayama seemed to be listening attentively, he had managed to slip a notebook from his pocket to be ready to write down any interesting bits of information from the old man's recollections. As one of his duties as a writer, he felt compelled to listen to the stories told by those who had lived in bygone days, no matter who they were, and to write them down for future generations. So whenever he came to Shimbashi, he made a point of stopping in here at the Obanaya.

The master was an ideal subject for his purposes, and from the old man's perspective, there was no better listener than Kurayama. Where, in this whole busy world, was he likely to find someone else willing to listen patiently and respectfully to an old man's complaints and boasts? So whenever Kurayama failed to appear after the accustomed interval, he would begin to worry that something might have happened to him.

The old man's name was Kitani Chōjirō. He had been born in 1848, the first year of the Kaei era, the son and heir of a minor retainer of the shogun who lived in the Kinshibori district in Honjo. He was a handsome boy, said to be the image of the famous actor Sanshō VIII, and if the world hadn't changed, he might have lived out his life like a character from one of the old romances. But in his twentieth year the shogun's regime collapsed, and Chōjirō lost his hereditary stipend. After several failures in the sorts of business ventures popular with impoverished samurai, he was left with no alternative but the world of entertainment. As a boy, he had enjoyed learning the art of storytelling, so he resolved to use this talent to make his living. He had the good fortune to be accepted as an apprentice by an old friend of his late father, a man named Ichizan, who was well known for his war tales. Receiving the name of Gozan, he took to the stage and, thanks to his natural eloquence and his handsome features, soon enjoyed considerable success. It was at this time that Jūkichi, the daughter of the Obanaya's proprietor, noticed him at a party where she had been called to perform. She proceeded to lavish her attentions on him and eventually made him her husband.

The couple had two sons. The old man had hoped to give a good education to his elder boy, Shōhachi, and see him turn into a man who could restore the family fortunes. But Shōhachi had been born into the world of the geisha, and by the time he started elementary school, he had already begun to show an affinity for the theater. At first, his father punished him severely in an effort to persuade him to give up these interests, occasionally even striking the boy. But in the end he gave in, deciding it was better to support his son in the hope of seeing him excel in his chosen profession. When Shōhachi was twelve years old, he was apprenticed to Ichikawa Danshū. He was given the stage name of Ichikawa Raishichi, and by the time he was twenty, after Danshū's death, Shōhachi's popularity had propelled him to the top of the bill and attracted the envy of his peers. But then, quite suddenly, he caught a cold that developed into acute pneumonia and his short life ended.

At the time, Shōhachi's younger brother, Takijirō, was about to graduate from middle school. Unfortunately, he was called in by the local police during a roundup of juvenile delinquents and given a warning that resulted in his expulsion from school. Nor did Chōjirō's troubles end there. Just as these events were driving him to despair of the future, a dispute broke out between the storytellers and the theater owners, and in a fit of rage against everyone and everything, he turned in his license as a performer.

The old man had never been an entertainer at heart, and his

stubborn nature had earned him the ill will of his fellow storytellers. In his own mind, he was reconciled to his lot, and it had always been his intention to avoid taking himself or the world too seriously. Nevertheless, quite unconsciously, his old arrogance and his preference for the past seemed to show through. While his master, Ichizan, was still alive, he had frequently been invited to banquets or geisha performances. But one day, at a housewarming party for a certain nouveau riche, he got carried away by his own eloquence and made some offensive remarks, ending the performance in disaster. After that, he flatly refused all invitations to appear at private parties, complaining that they involved too many restrictions, and he devoted himself to his career in the variety halls. If a performer didn't have the liberty to speak his mind as he could on the stage, then what was the point? And if the upper crust wanted to hear Gozan tell his tales, then they could come to the theater like everyone else. Whether he was performing for common laborers or the high and mighty, he was not one to alter his act. So, like the old master Fūryū Shidōken, the older he got, the livelier his performances became as he insulted his audiences and provoked them to laughter at the same time. In the end, his popularity was such that even during the slow months of February and August, when the variety halls usually were empty, he always drew a respectable crowd. Kurayama Nansō's friendship with the old man sprang from the fact that he had so regularly attended these performances.

"Do you think you'll go back on the stage someday? Since you gave it up, I haven't been to the halls myself."

"Somehow I don't think I could. Not with the world the way it's become. No one wants to sit still long enough to listen to the old stories any more."

"I suppose you're right. It's 'moving pictures' they want now."

"The *gidayū* balladeers, the comedians—all the acts at the variety halls are out of fashion."

"But it's not just the variety halls. It's the same with the theaters. If you think about it, I suppose it's inevitable: no one goes to see or hear a particular kind of performance any more. The truth is, they don't care what they're watching as long as it's cheap and simple and they can get it all in one spot . . . which can only mean the movies."

"You're right. As you say, people today don't want to take the time and trouble to appreciate the actor's or storyteller's art. The stories themselves sell well enough in print, but the halls are empty. But I don't think much of phonograph recordings of performances or those books that transcribe them. Sensei, don't you think that art should come from the passion that overtakes the artist in the act of creation? It's that enthusiasm the viewer feels and perhaps even shares. That's the real mystery of art—it exists only in the meeting of minds between the artist and his audience. Wouldn't you agree?" The reactionary old storyteller and the outdated novelist wet their throats with cold, bitter tea and were about to go on with their flights of fancy when the reed screen parted, and Jūkichi, the mistress of the Obanaya, entered the room.

"How nice to see you!" she said. She was a short, plump old woman, but there was no trace in her of the brashness one often sees in the mistresses of *machiai* or restaurants, the kind of fat women who flatter you shamelessly in person but savage you the minute your back is turned. Anyone could see from her pleasant face, with its round eyes and chubby cheeks, that she was an honest, good-hearted woman. Dressed as she was in a kimono of finely patterned silk gauze fastened with a satin obi, it was obvious that she was returning from an engagement. But there was an old-fashioned dignity in her manner and style of dress that seemed more typical of a teacher of Katōbushi ballad singing than a Shimbashi geisha. She was the most agreeable sort of woman, and neither the older geisha nor the saucy younger girls ever had a bad word to say about her. All the older women of the quarter, Jūkichi's peers, were geisha of influence who were accorded the title of "Madam nee-san." But Jūkichi never took it upon herself to comment on their activities, right or wrong, and always left such matters to the officials in the geisha association—who, in turn, considered her to be a very sensible and dependable woman. On the other hand, she also was admired by the malcontents, women who would have liked to have influence in the association but did not, as well as by the independent geisha who, no longer young but not yet senior, were caught in the awkward position of being simply "nee-san." All these women appreciated Jūkichi for her openness and her generosity, but a number of them wished that she would speak her mind more freely from time to time. At her age, however, Jūkichi no longer saw the need to hold office in the association or take the lead in organizing the seasonal performances or dance recitals just to ensure the success of the girls at the Obanaya. Of course, had her elder boy, Shōhachi, lived and become a great actor, or had her younger boy, Takijirō, graduated from school and had prospects ahead of him, she would have worked feverishly to put money aside for them. But one was dead and the other had turned out badly, having effectively been disowned and banished from the house—and so Jūkichi had resigned herself to quietly living out the time that remained to her in the company of her husband. Furthermore, her house had enjoyed such a good reputation since the early days of the Shimbashi quarter that she often had requests from girls wanting to be taken in; and in addition she still had calls for engagements from her old, reliable customers. So there was no lack of business from day to day. Still, no matter how hard she tried to drive them from her thoughts, her sons were always on her mind.

Jūkichi knelt quietly in front of the family altar and recited her prayers. When she was finished, she extinguished the candles and closed the doors of the cabinet. Returning to the front room, she changed into a summer kimono of dappled cotton and was chatting with the old attendant who managed the accounts when her husband came out with Kurayama to see him off.

"Sensei, are you leaving already?" she said. "Can't you stay a bit longer?"

"No, but I'll stop by again soon."

"But I was hoping you'd go over the Amigasa song with me."

"All the more reason I have to go!" Kurayama laughed. "I'm afraid I haven't been practicing very diligently. Please give my regards to the master when you see him."

"Well then, do hurry back."

Jūkichi and her husband returned to the sitting room. She lit her pipe. "Dear, is Komayo upstairs?" she said in a pointed sort of way.

"No, she went out a little while ago."

"I didn't know a thing about it . . . but it seems that Rikiji's patron has been asking for her at the Hamazaki."

"Is that so?" the old man said, rubbing a cloth over the tobacco case he had made from the skin of a dried citron.

"I ran into Rikiji a few days ago, and she said some things that sounded a bit odd, but I didn't think anything of it. Then tonight I heard the whole story from a guest, and it all started to make sense."

"Well, Komayo certainly has more nerve than you'd imagine from looking at her."

"But people might think I was secretly playing go-between. I don't like it."

"Still, you don't want to speak out of turn. Just let it be. If she'd talked to you beforehand, you might have said something. But she went behind your back, and what's done is done. Girls these days seem capable of anything, and it's not as though Komayo's the only one. None of them seems to have the slightest notion of what loyalty means—that's what makes them so carefree wherever they go."

"You're right. I heard an earful this evening. There even was talk about paying off her debt. It seems he's offered to buy her contract and take care of her, but she hasn't given him a definite answer."

"She's had so many engagements lately—maybe she has bigger things in mind."

"Well, as long as she goes on earning money for the house,

that's all we can ask. But no one stays young forever, and if someone's making an offer like that, she'd do well to listen."

"But where does the man come from? Is he an aristocrat?"

"I told you, he's Rikiji's patron."

"Yes, but what sort of man is he?"

"Don't you know him, dear? He's with one of those insurance companies. In his late thirties, certainly under forty; he's a handsome man with a moustache."

"So she's found herself a prize. But with business so good, it's no wonder she doesn't want to give it up. Now that she's got such a fine patron, all she has to do is take a lover—an actor, perhaps, like Kikugoro or Kichiemon—and she can have her cake and eat it too." Gozan laughed.

"You really are incorrigible." Tapping her pipe on the ashtray, she gave him a disapproving look, but there was no anger in her eyes. The phone rang in the front room.

"I suppose there's no one to answer it," Jūkichi said, getting wearily to her feet.

5. A Dream in the Daylight

It was late August and the drought had grown so serious that there were rumors the water supply would be cut off temporarily. Then suddenly one evening, a torrential rain began to fall, continuing all night and halfway through the next day. When at last the skies cleared, the season had changed. Autumn, which had arrived so abruptly, could plainly be felt in the brilliant color of the sky and the leaves of the willows, in the clatter of geta and the ringing of *rikisha* bells in the streets at night; and crickets had begun to chirp busily in the alley dustbins.

Komayo had been planning to go with Yoshioka-san to a hot spring resort like Hakone or Shuzenji, but the deluge had damaged train lines out of the city, and so she persuaded him to stay at the Sanshun'en in Morigasaki. The Sanshun'en was a villa belonging to the *machiai* in Kobiki-chō known as the Taigetsu, the preeminent establishment in Shimbashi, and as such, it did not open its rooms to just anyone. In an excess of prosperity, the mistress of the Taigetsu had originally built the villa for her own amusement. But greedy by nature, she could never abide the idea of such a large and elegant building standing empty much of the time, and so leaving the management of the main house in Kobiki-chō to her adoptive daughter and some trustworthy maids, she turned the Sanshun'en into a branch establishment. She then spread the word among her most faithful customers and the geisha who frequented her *machiai* that they could bring their guests here for amorous adventures. Customers at the villa never ran the risk of meeting other guests, as they would at a normal inn, and this atmosphere of privacy and pampering was rewarded with exceptionally large tips. The prestige of the Taigetsu in Shimbashi made the geisha feel that attracting a customer to the villa would increase their standing in the quarter. Thus it was not unusual for one of them to show up at the *machiai* with a gift she had brought back from her stay at the villa and proudly express her thanks for the reception she had received. There was undoubtedly something of this in Komayo's determination to go there with Yoshioka.

It was after ten o'clock when the maid cleared away the breakfast trays. Wisps of cloud covered the early autumn sky, and from time to time the breeze shook loose drops of dew from the petals of the bush clover at the end of the veranda. The insects beneath, however, seemed undisturbed, continuing the same quiet trilling they had kept up all night.

Komayo had fashioned a nightgown by wrapping a narrow sash around the light summer kimono she wore after the bath. She had fastened her hair in a casual knot at the back of her head and was stretched out on her stomach, a Shikishima cigarette dangling from her lips as she glanced at the *Miyako* newspaper the maid had brought in. Yawning slightly, she looked up at Yoshioka.

"It's lovely here," she said, her voice sounding a bit forced. "So peaceful."

Yoshioka, a cigar clutched in his teeth, had been studying her for some time, admiring the look of dishevelment left by sleep, but now he sat up to answer her.

"That's just the point. It's nice living quietly like this. So isn't it about time you gave up being a geisha?" She smiled brightly at him but said nothing. "Well? Why don't you quit? Don't you trust me?"

"It's not that I don't trust you. . . ."

"Then you don't think I'm serious?"

"But it would never work. You've got Rikiji to think about and the mistress at the Murasakiya in Hama-chō. It might be fine for a while, but before long you'd make me suffer, too."

"You know I've practically broken off with Rikiji. How can you still talk about her after everything I said last night? As for the other one, I'm really under no obligation to her. But if they bother you so much, perhaps we should forget the whole thing."

"Now don't be angry," she cried, her tone changing abruptly at his harsh words. She buried her face in his chest like a baby seeking its mother's breast, ignoring the way her robe had come apart in front.

The sensation of the woman's cool hair and hot brow brushing across his bare skin sent a shiver through Yoshioka, and the warmth and weight of her body on his knees worked its way slowly to the core of his being. He could feel this rich sensation drawing him into a pleasant trance, and he fought to stay awake after the long, sleepless night. Once again he gazed at the disheveled figure sprawled across his lap, and he was seized by an overwhelming desire to make her his own, not just her body but her heart and her soul as well.

It struck him as wonderfully strange that this woman, whom he had abandoned without much thought when he had gone abroad, should have such a hold on him now. That evening in early summer when he ran into her at the Imperial Theater and then called her to the Hamazaki in Tsukiji had begun as just a night's adventure, an attempt to recapture the excitement of his student days. But one night had led to another and then still others, and before he realized what was happening, he was overcome by the need to possess Komayo, every inch of her.

How odd. He had never meant things to turn out this way. . . . And yet when he saw her face, he could feel his heart leap—a heart that was perhaps not as free as he had thought. For years, he had amused himself with women, but he had never once felt such a strange emotion. Ever since his student days he'd had a reputation for being methodical, perhaps even a bit stiff and unfeeling. In those days there were those who faulted him for his abrupt manner. When he went with friends to a noodle shop or a steak house, he hated to be treated or to treat others and always insisted on dividing the bill down to the last sen. So at about that time, when he first began buying the services of geisha, he had done so it in the same spirit of reason and clarity. Rather than suppress his sexual desire only to risk shaming himself by falling under the spell of a maid or some other amateur, it was far safer to spend the money to buy a woman properly when needed. To pay for a woman and have her without undue worry to relieve his sexual tension and then pass his examinations with high marks—this was combining duty with pleasure and, he thought, killing two birds with one stone. For a young man of the modern age, in whom there was no trace of the Confucian values that had shaped earlier generations, the only thing that mattered was success, reaching his goal, and he'd had neither the inclination nor the leisure to question the means that got him there. Nor indeed had there been anything to feel guilty about: it was simply the inevitable tendency of the times. Yoshioka had known about what it would cost to pay for each month's amusements, and he had budgeted accordingly. Then if his expenditures were less than the amount he had set aside for this purpose, he would give the difference to his current woman without stinting. But if he had exceeded his budget, he would refuse her requests, no matter how many letters she sent asking him to visit.

His pattern was much the same after he came home from his time abroad and began his career. The reason that he had become the patron of Rikiji of the Minatoya had nothing to do with love or even sexual attraction; it was motivated entirely by his desire to be known as a man of the moment. It was rumored in the quarter that the statesman Itō Shumpo had become involved with Rikiji the year before, and even now she was in the habit of alluding to this dalliance with very little prompting. As a result, Rikiji herself had begun acting as though she had suddenly become a lady of great quality, taking lessons in the tea ceremony and koto and even trying to learn calligraphy and painting. As a young man of affairs recently launched in life, Yoshioka knew that the cost of becoming the patron of a geisha would be the same whether he chose the best or the worst of them. If that were the case and since he rather liked the idea of surprising people by having his name appear in the gossip columns of the *Miyako*, he began courting Rikiji with unaccustomed extravagance. At the time, she had a reputation for being haughty; nevertheless, Yoshioka's good looks and liberal spending won her over with unexpected ease. But Rikiji was three years older than Yoshioka, and even though she was universally recognized as a geisha of the first class, when she went out in her black, crested kimono and white collar, in more ordinary dress and without makeup, she somehow looked like a spiteful middle-aged matron, and the tiny wrinkles and dark circles around her eyes, her broad forehead, and her large mouth were noticeable. Also, from the beginning, Yoshioka had implicitly acknowledged her superior position, so he had never felt entirely free to do as he might have liked, despite the fact that he was technically her patron. He even wondered from time to time whether she wasn't mocking her "young master," and he sometimes imagined what it would be like to have a slightly younger, more alluring woman, the kind who could give herself completely to a man. As for the teahouse maid he had set up as the mistress of the Murasakiya in Hama-chō—more or less to be rid of her—he had always found a reason to avoid a final break. But now, by chance, he was reunited with Komayo, the woman of his student days, and they had achieved an intimacy that seemed both powerful and quite natural. Since they had known each other for so long, he felt no constraints on what he said or did when he was with her. Moreover, she was a beautiful woman in full flower with whom he could be proud to be seen. So he'd hit upon a plan: he was determined to pay off her debt and make her his mistress and then install her in the house he'd always hoped to build near Kamakura where, in the days to come, he would relax with her on the weekends.

When he told her that he was building her a villa and wanted to hold a grand party to celebrate having ransomed her from the profession, he thought she would accept immediately. So when she refused to give him any clear answer at all, part of him was angry at the slight while another part was dismayed at the thought of letting such a jewel slip between his fingers. After that, he decided that he would make one last attempt to under-stand what was going on inside her, why she had refused him; and if there was nothing he could do, he would end the affair in the name of masculine pride. But now, lost in contemplation of her loose, rounded chignon, more that of a wife than a geisha, and the thin kimono held together by nothing but a narrow sash, he couldn't help feeling the unmistakable regret that she was not his mistress, that they were not sitting together in the new villa.

He had become very fond of this hairstyle on Komayo. He had first seen her this way the fourth or fifth time he called for her. She had been paying a sick call to a sister geisha and had come directly to the teahouse with her hair like this and her kimono tucked in at the waist like any other woman's. The effect was completely different from her usual appearance as a geisha, with her high-piled *tsubushi*, or gingko-leaf hairstyle, and long, flowing kimono. There was something new and refreshing about it, something that reminded him of the *onnagata* actor Kawai, who appeared in the new-style theater, and it aroused in him stronger feelings than anything he had ever felt with the utterly professional Rikiji, much less with the mistress of the Murasaki, whose ways could be plodding and at times almost crude. From the first time he had seen this Komayo, he had been filled with a desire to keep her this way; and each time he called for her, each time they spent the night together, the desire grew more and more difficult to restrain.

"You're heavy!" he said at last, trying to shake her from his lap, but Komayo pressed her face more tightly against his chest.

"It's so nice here," she murmured, her voice like that of a spoiled child. "And I'm so tired. I didn't sleep a wink last night." She looked up at him.

"And whose fault is that?"

"I'm so unhappy," she said, her tone suddenly pathetic, "I really am." She slid her hand up to his chest and gave him a hard pinch.

It was one of the foolish little tricks peculiar to women of her trade, a special art they alone practiced. When at a loss as to how to respond to a man, they would resort to these distracting ruses, each one using her own particular ploy—though it's a mystery when and how they were learned. As a rule, the man was thrown off balance by the trick, tipped toward the edge of his resistance, while the woman, taking advantage of his confusion, often found the situation resolved to her satisfaction. Nor was Yoshioka unfamiliar with the game. As a veteran of the pleasure quarters, he had seen demonstrations of this form of coquetry from many different women. One might whimper for a time before throwing herself at his mercy, while another would feign arrogance and end by giving in entirely. A third might choose to play the fool, offering a display of high spirits. But whatever the ruse, the woman would use it to work herself into a state of excitement, almost as if she were getting drunk; and the man, even if he found her too brazen, would end up being taken in. The effect was unforgettable, and on occasion Yoshioka found himself teasing or tormenting his current woman just to bring on her repertoire of tricks.

They pinched and tickled each other now like animals at play, and for the moment at least, Komayo was able to forget his proposal to ransom her.

But the respite was, of course, only temporary. She knew that she soon would be forced to give him a definite answer. If she equivocated too long, it would be the same as refusing him. If she refused him, she would be losing more than just a good customer; in her present circumstances, she would be losing a great deal indeed. But on the other hand, were she to give up her profession and become a kept woman and then find herself abandoned, she would be faced with the terrible prospect of having to return to the quarter a third time. What she really wanted was to remain a geisha but continue to enjoy Yoshioka's patronage. She had spent much of her sleepless night trying to come up with a plan he would find plausible. If he paid her debt and set her up in business for herself, she would promise to foreswear entertaining at *machiai* and observe a strict ten o'clock curfew even at the teahouses. But Yoshioka already was familiar with the role of the *danna* and knew from long experience with Rikiji the considerable expense involved. At this point, it wasn't likely he would find the prospect amusing. But then again, if she intended to remain a geisha, there was no real need to be set up on her own.

"Well, think it over then for a few days. As long as we're here, you should consider it."

Having worked straight through the summer, Yoshioka was taking this week of vacation in early autumn, and he was anxious to persuade Komayo during their time together. For his purposes, he needed a place where they could be alone, and in that sense the Sanshun'en was preferable to a hot spring resort in Hakone or Shuzenji. He was determined to take advantage of this opportunity, so when a call came from Eda in the morning on the third day summoning him back to Tokyo to attend to a stock transaction, he promised to return by evening at the latest. So she wouldn't have to be alone while she waited for him, he summoned two of her sister geisha before he left, Hanasuke from Komayo's own house and Chiyomatsu from another establishment.

When Komayo returned alone to their room, she sat down in a heap, bent her head toward the tatami, and burst into tears. She was so upset and confused. For two days and nights now she had wanted to run away but had no idea where to go. He had pressed her to give him an answer, badgered her so relentlessly that she was no longer able to be agreeable. She was exhausted and her head was throbbing; and when she thought about the prospect of being here another two or three days, the Sanshun'en, which had been her idea in the first place, seemed little better than a prison.

Somewhere, a rooster began to crow. To her ears, it was the sound of the country, and suddenly all the sadness and hardship she'd suffered during her days in distant Akita came flooding back. The rooster fell silent and crows began to caw in its place. The insects were humming beyond the veranda. She couldn't stand it any longer. If she continued to hesitate, she might never be able to return to Shimbashi. But why was she so fond of Shimbashi? Why did she feel so at home there? Although she was still dressed in her nightclothes, she suddenly, with no other thought than to get away, ran out into the corridor—even though she had no idea which way to go except toward the bath.

There she immediately found herself face to face with someone who seemed even more surprised than she was: a handsome man in a cotton kimono. Fan in hand, he apparently was out for a stroll through what he thought was a deserted villa. He was in his late twenties, of average build, and from his shaved, penciled eyebrows and cropped hair, it was clear that he was an actor. It was the *onnagata* known as Segawa Isshi.

"Oh, nii-san!" she said.

"Komayo? You gave me a terrible start," said Isshi, making a show of raising his hand to his chest as if to calm himself. He drew a deep breath.

Komayo had known him from the time she had made her debut in Shimbashi, when they both had studied Hanayanagi dance with the same teacher. In those days he had been a mere apprentice. But when she had returned to the quarter and met him again last spring, in the dressing room during a special performance by the Shimbashi geisha at the Kabukiza, he was already a celebrated actor, known to the geisha as *nii-san*, their elder brother. Meeting him so unexpectedly now, just as she'd run out in her gown, distraught and on the point of fleeing the villa, she felt the joy of a traveler in a distant land running into someone from her hometown. She suddenly felt reassured and her loneliness seemed to dissipate. In her joy, she was on the verge of throwing herself into his arms.

"Nii-san, I'm sorry if I frightened you."

"My heart's still pounding. Here, see for yourself," he said, casually taking her hand and pressing it to his chest.

Komayo blushed. "I'm so sorry."

"That's all right. And I'll soon pay you back."

"But nii-san, I said I'm sorry. And it was your fault anyway, standing there so quietly."

Still holding her hand, Isshi studied her disheveled hair and robe. Because his engagement at the Meiji Theater had ended the day before, he explained, he had agreed to meet a few friends here to play cards, but for some reason they hadn't shown up yet.

"What fun you must be having!" she said.

"What do you mean?"

"I mean, with whoever came with you. If you want me to keep quiet, I expect a treat when we get back to Tokyo."

"I'd say it's the other way around. It's *your* secret rendezvous I shouldn't have barged in on like this."

Realizing he was about to leave her, Komayo began to feel tearful again. "I'm so miserable," she said, taking his sleeve. "Please—have pity on me."

"Why don't we meet later? I assume you're staying the night."

"But there's no one with me here. I've been left all alone."

"Then it's just the two of us. The lady of the house has gone to the beach on an errand."

"Is that so? She's gone, too?"

The thought that the large house was empty made it seem even lonelier. The garden in the rear, visible through the windows off the corridor, baked in the lingering heat of the sun. No sound could be heard, inside or out, not even the comings and goings beyond the fence—not a murmur except the droning of the cicadas and the other insects.

They stood there for a moment in silence, looking at each other.

"Isn't it quiet," he remarked.

"It certainly is."

"Komayo, my dear. What would you do if I had evil intentions? There's no one here to come to your rescue."

"Nii-san, don't frighten me," she said, clinging to him.

When the two geisha who had been summoned from Tokyo arrived by taxi to keep her company, they found Komayo in bed, looking as though she might indeed have fallen victim to someone's evil intentions. They glanced at each other but said nothing.

6. *The Actor's Seal*

While the sun was still high in the sky, Yoshioka returned to the Sanshun'en, bringing the plump, saké-loving Eda with him. Eda had planned to take the late train back to Tokyo, but Komayo insisted that he stay and spend the night in their room. So until past midnight, she fluttered about, serving them whiskey and drinking a great deal herself, to the point that even Eda got annoyed. In the end, she was sick, bringing up everything she'd drunk and creating a general scene. The next day she spent with a bag of ice on her head. This display left Yoshioka dumbfounded, and deciding there was nothing further he could do for the moment, he beat a retreat from the villa. But Komayo's indisposal had been partly an act, as she'd been planning all along to go back to Shimbashi and, from there, head straight for the Shinjuku Inari Shrine, in whose powers she was a great believer. She wanted to ask the oracle whether she would be taking too great a risk in giving up her profession immediately to entrust herself to Yoshioka's care. Even if things went well for a time, wasn't there always the chance that they would end badly, just as they had before? She had decided to consult the oracle and then talk to Jūkichi and the mistress of the Hamazaki before giving Yoshioka an answer.

Komayo had just returned from the public bath and was kneeling in front of her mirror stand to fix her hair when Hanako, the apprentice geisha, came running up the stairs.

"Komayo-san, you have an engagement."

"Oh dear! I suppose it's the Hamazaki again."

She imagined that Yoshioka, who had left the Sanshun'en by car only a short time earlier, must have gone directly to Tsukiji without returning home and was already calling for her.

"No, it's at the Gishun."

"The Gishun? That's odd. Are you sure it isn't a mistake?" Komayo cocked her head to one side and let out a sigh of relief. Since she had never been to the Gishun *machiai* before, she asked Hanako to decline, saying that her hair wasn't done and that she was feeling a bit tired and was going to rest. But before long there was another call, begging her to come just as she was, if only for a few minutes. When she asked who the customer was, she was informed that it was a "friend," though that told her little. Still, it would be too rude simply to refuse, and so feeling reluctant and a bit apprehensive, she found herself in a *rikisha* making her way down a row of large and small *machiai* that lined an alley behind the Ministry of Agriculture and Commerce.

The Gishun was marked by a sign in Saga-style characters and a wicker gate. Told to go immediately to the second floor, she warily climbed the stairs. It was still daytime and the reed door stood open. Down the length of the hall she could see a room and a lone figure leaning against the pillar of the alcove, plucking at a shamisen. It was none other than Segawa, the man from her encounter at the Sanshun'en.

She let out a little cry of surprise and stood in the doorway for a moment, so lost in joy and embarrassment that she couldn't bring herself to enter the room.

Two days ago, in broad daylight, there in the corridor of the deserted villa, something had happened. She couldn't say who had taken the initiative or who had done what, but she knew that it had been a delightful interlude. Since the man in question was an immensely popular actor, she had assumed it had been no more than the sport of the moment and would end where it began. But even if it had been no more than that, it would have been the greatest treat a geisha could enjoy—and now suddenly, before the third day had passed, here he was, calling her in secret to a *machiai*. This showed a consideration beyond anything she could have imagined, and she found herself speechless as her eyes filled with tears of happiness.

He had been playing "I Wait Alone," no doubt on purpose, and now he left the shamisen resting on his knees as he motioned for her to approach. "It's cooler here. Come and sit with me."

"Thank you," she murmured almost inaudibly, her eyes staring at the floor like a maiden meeting her prospective husband for the first time.

Segawa was utterly delighted by her confusion and at the same time began to feel an unexpected curiosity. He had never imagined that a geisha could seem so innocent and yet so serious. At her age—twenty-four or twenty-five, he would guess—she must have known an actor or two. But somehow the bit of fun that they had had the day before yesterday at the Sanshun'en had developed into something that he could no longer simply drop or pretend had never happened; and so he had called her here, half from what might be termed his "professional duty" as an actor and half from a need to make it up to her. Once she arrived and discovered who was waiting for her, he was sure that she'd be quite at ease and have some quick remark—"Aren't we the persistent one"—at the ready. But now that he saw this completely unexpected reaction, these clear signs that Komayo's emotions were involved, his masculine vanity was aroused and he was filled with delight that their little adventure could have such significant results. It amused him to consider the various ways he might proceed with the affair, and he found himself thinking how he would employ all his skills as a lover to lead her on, everything he had learned from past experience.

For her part, Komayo felt as though she'd become lost in a dream. She could neither speak nor move, as if she'd been bewitched by a fox, but she was filled with an overwhelming sense of elation and gratitude.

Some time later, Segawa, meticulous as ever, found himself casually helping Komayo straighten her hair and clothing. Then he made sure his own appearance was impeccable before seating himself by the window in the next room where the breeze was cool. The wooden clappers of the night watchman sounded in the distance. Apparently it was past ten o'clock.

"Koma-chan, would you pour me a cup of tea?"

"It's gotten cold. I'll go and get a fresh pot." She rose obligingly, but he took her hand.

"No, leave it. We don't want the maid coming in."

"I suppose not," she said. Her hand still in his, she fell back to her knees and leaned against him. "But I'm thirsty, too, even though I didn't have much to drink earlier." They shared the cold dregs of the tea from the same cup.

"Koma-chan, please—promise to meet me again soon."

"Nii-san! Of course! And you promise, too. If you ask me, I'll do anything to see you again."

"If my mother weren't so difficult, we could spend the night here. But I suppose it's not possible."

"Probably not. But when will I see you again? I'm always free after eleven o'clock."

"But we don't want to be reckless and have your *danna* find out. We've got to be careful."

"It's all right, he almost never stays the night. But it probably will be more difficult for you."

"No, if I want to spend the night out, I certainly can. Except that my mother's such a nuisance, which is odd, since she was in the business herself. But Koma-chan, let's meet tomorrow night. My rehearsal should be over by eight or nine, and I'll come here straight from the theater. Would that suit you? Or do you know somewhere even more discreet?"

"No, that's fine. But if I get a call I can't refuse, promise you'll wait for me."

"I promise," Segawa said, taking her hand quite formally as if he were a young man just starting out in the pleasure quarters. "And now I'll have them call me a *rikisha*."

While they waited for it to come, Segawa went on talking to her sweetly. Komayo saw him off and paid her respects to the management of the house; but then, realizing she'd forgotten to call a ride for herself, she walked out into the early autumn night. The stars were brilliant and the cool breeze played with the locks of hair that had come loose at her temples. Passing in front of the ministry building, Komayo headed for the Izumo Bridge, the soles of her wooden clogs clattering on the pavement. As she reviewed the events of the evening, she found herself gazing across the bridge at the lights of the Ginza in the distance. Without quite knowing why, she turned away and wandered off into the deserted streets in search of a place to lose herself in her thoughts.

Everything suddenly seemed changed. The lights in the upstairs windows of the *machiai* she passed, the musicians in the street, everything she heard or saw was somehow new. It never occurred to her to wonder whether there were other women in Segawa's life. She simply was too happy. Had she chosen to live out her days in the quiet backwater of Akita, she would never have known this kind of joy—a thought that made her grateful for all the trials she had endured and made her wonder at the strange turns of human destiny. She felt as though she were understanding for the first time what it truly meant to be a geisha, all the sorrow and the joy. It was odd, though: she'd been a geisha yesterday, too, and yet somehow everything was different now. She had a new lover, a famous actor with countless admirers, and her reputation as a geisha was made. She had suddenly risen in status and dignity, and the thought filled her with elation.

Just then, a geisha's *rikisha* passed her in the street. Komayo glanced at the girl, wondering where she might be from. If she turns here under the lamp to look at me, Komayo thought, I will stare right back—such was her newfound confidence.

7. *Afterglow*

When the setting sun sank low over the roofs of the houses in Komparu Street and shone in through the blinds in the windows of the upper floor of the Obanaya, the maid would call from the foot of the stairs, "The bath is hot!" Upstairs, the geisha lay sprawled on the tatami mats: Komayo in a summer kimono made of toweling tied with a narrow sash; Kikuchiyo in a cotton nightdress; Hanasuke in a bleached cotton shirt and underskirt. With the apprentice, Hanako, and Otsuru, the young girl who had just begun her training, they were five in all.

Kikuchiyo was short and plump. She was twenty-two or perhaps twenty-three years old and was known to the others as "Goldfish," a nickname that suited her round face and eyes, her flattened nose, and her short, thick neck. In sum, she could hardly have been called pretty, but her skin, visible in all its glory through the thin material of her nightgown, was wonderfully smooth, and there was something in her tiny chin and white throat that seemed to invite a caressing hand, like a languid cat. She invariably wore her hair in the flattened Shimada style, with a thick application of oil and pads at the front and sides to keep the shape she wanted. Even on the hottest days, her makeup was so thick that it threatened to peel away from her face, and her taste in kimono was gaudy, to say the least. As a result, malicious people said she looked like a tart when she appeared at her engagements, but it made her look younger and thus attracted the best clients.

Hanasuke, the geisha clad only in her underrobe, was a solidly built woman with curly hair and dark eyes in a broad, swarthy face. Although she was almost the same age as Komayo, anyone looking at her would have taken her to be at least thirty—as she herself knew only too well. In fact, knowing that her looks and style could never compete with those of the thousand other geisha in Shimbashi, she had found a strategy that was appropriate to her station. When she appeared at an engagement, she worked even harder than the maids; and when she was in the company of younger and prettier geisha, she adopted a humble demeanor in the hope of being asked along to future engagements. As a result, she was well liked by the other women and kept relatively busy at the teahouses. Furthermore, for the past two or three years she'd had a patron, a moneylender who, oddly enough, found her plainness reassuring. Consequently, she had no worries about money and went about with her postal savings book tucked in her kimono like an amulet.

Hanako and Otsuru, who had been rehearsing a duet from *Osome*, began putting away their shamisen. Kikuchiyo, careful not to disturb her coiffure, indulged herself in an enormous and unattractive yawn, while Hanasuke rose from the futon and stretched. The four women pulled combs from their dressing stands and pinned up their hair for the bath, but Komayo, still stretched out facing the wall, made no move to join them.

"What time is it? Is the bath made already?"

"Get up or we'll tickle you."

"I'm sorry, but you'll have to get permission."

"Permission! Who from? You're amazing."

"But she's been acting funny since yesterday, and last night she was talking in her sleep. It was so loud I thought someone else was in the room."

"Really?" said Komayo, her expression suggesting that she herself was surprised that things had gone so far. She sat up with an effort. "Well then, I owe you a treat."

"So something has happened, hasn't it?"

"Don't jump to conclusions. I'm just grateful for everything you did the other day at the Sanshun'en."

"Come on, you can't fool us."

"But I'd had nearly a whole bottle of whiskey. My head's still fuzzy."

"Koma-chan, what are you up to? Jūkichi hasn't said anything, but even she seems to be worried about you."

"Actually, I don't know what to do. I don't want to ruin things with you-know-who, but I also can't have people saying I'm about to be bought off and leave the quarter. I'm fed up with the whole business."

"Are you meeting him this evening?"

"No, I haven't heard from him since then, but I'm sure he'll turn up soon. And I still have no idea what to tell him."

There were footsteps on the stairs. It was Osada, the attendant, a slim woman in her midforties whose large eyes, fine nose, and oval face might have attracted attention in her youth. Even now, although her hair was thinning and turning prematurely white in front, her whole appearance—from the way she wore her kimono to the complexion damaged by too many years of heavy powder—suggested that she'd got her start as a courtesan in the Susaki licensed quarter. She had been married for a time, but when her husband died more than seven years ago, a placement agency had found her a position as a maid at the Obanaya. She'd watched and waited, learning all about the job of the attendant, and when the previous woman had been fired for some impropriety three years earlier, Osada had stepped in.

Komayo looked a little startled at the sight of her, thinking she'd come to announce Yoshioka's summons. "Osada-san, is it for me?" she blurted out.

"No, Kikuchiyo had a call from the Shimpuku. Your party at the Midoriya is at six o'clock, so you can go afterward." The remark was something between a suggestion and an order, and she went on without waiting for an answer. "And the kimono from yesterday should do, don't you think?"

Kikuchiyo said nothing but hurried down the stairs to the bath.

There was no real bad blood between Kikuchiyo and Komayo. Still, Komayo's arrival had clearly thrown the more senior woman off balance. Komayo had come the year before, just as Kikuchiyo had completed her contract and been promoted to a position of seniority with a share in the house's profits. She had established herself as an influential geisha with two important patrons, one a department head at a ministry and the other a wealthy member of parliament from the provinces. But the success of a latecomer like Komayo still bothered her, and it showed in her behavior. For her part, Komayo had come to despise Kikuchiyo, finding her haughty ways inappropriate to such a plain woman. Caught between the two was the homely but clever Hanasuke, who made it a rule never to take sides but played up to both women in order to be asked along to their engagements. Still, Komayo was closer to her own age and had suffered similar trials, and so they tended to share confidences. Hanasuke had originally worked in Yoshichō. Her contract had been purchased by a man who set her up as his mistress, but three years ago, when he abandoned her, she'd been forced to make a second debut, this time in Shimbashi.

The details of her story emerged when Komayo had turned to her for advice, soon after Yoshioka had begun to talk of paying off Komayo's debt. Hanasuke's attitude was that men were fine when things were going well, but once they had a change of heart, they could be terribly cruel. This sentiment fitted nicely with Komayo's long-standing theory that men were fickle by nature, and from that time on the two women began to compare notes more frequently. Ultimately, they decided that the best plan was to put away as much as they possibly could while they still had earning power and thereby accumulate the resources that would allow them to live comfortably, perhaps running a small business of some sort, and have nothing further to do with men.

After she left her husband's family in Akita, there was little else for Komayo to do except return to her life as a geisha. But living for six or seven years as a married woman, especially in such a remote corner of the country, had made her prone to feel discouraged and slow to change her mood. So now, despite her best intentions to be lively and cheerful for her engagements, to put up with almost anything if it meant securing a wealthy client, when she found herself at the teahouse, she was no longer able to throw herself into the work, no longer willing to be as agreeable and compligant as she had been in her youth. She bristled at the overbearing manner of teahouse maids and at *machiai* mistresses who were constantly trying to push her into the arms of their clients. In fact, up to this point, she had never spent the night with any of them except Yoshioka. Hanasuke, however, speaking as if the problem were her own, told Komayo that she would regret it later if she didn't earn as much as she could now. "If I only had your looks . . . ," she added, her voiced filled with envy. Komayo, however, felt no particular need to add to her earnings in this way and, as a result, lacked the courage to do so. But now, in one evening, both the need and the courage seemed to well up inside her.

After Kikuchiyo's noisy departure for her engagement at the Shimpuku, the two women had a leisurely bath and then moved their makeup stands away from the last rays of sunlight filtering through the front window. They put them side by side under the small window that looked out on the drying rack at the rear, and they had just begun to apply their makeup when Komayo suddenly spoke up.

"Hana-chan, are you still seeing that man?"

"Which one?" Hanasuke murmured, concentrating on securing the unruly curls at her temples.

"You know, the one who was always at the Chiyomoto just after I came here, when we were having a lot of engagements together."

"That group with Sugishima-san . . . ?"

"That's it, Sugishima-san. Who were those men? Politicians?"

Komayo had been staring intently into the mirror combing her hair, when suddenly, for no apparent reason, she remembered the ruddy face of the man named Sugishima, a customer who had requested her for several engagements around the time she had come back to the quarter and who had done his best to seduce her. If worse came to worst and her relationship with Yoshioka-san were damaged by her refusal to quit the profession, then, whether she wanted to or not, she would have to find someone to replace him in order to be able to continue her affair with Segawa. So now she found herself going over the names of all the customers who had propositioned her in the past.

"I think he's from Dairen. At any rate, he has some sort of business in China."

"Is that so? Then he doesn't live here?"

"He comes at the New Year and during the summer. But now that you mention it, I didn't see him this past summer. I asked him to bring me some Nanjin satin and some silk crepe. I always place an order when he goes—it's good quality and quite cheap."

"Really? Then I should have ordered something myself. But I didn't like the man, so pushy and vulgar somehow."

"He took a real fancy to you. He wanted me to arrange things, said that he'd do anything. I can't remember such an awkward evening."

"It was just after I'd come back, and I didn't know how to behave. I suppose I didn't really know what was going on."

"He does seem like a bore to look at him, but they say he can be quite kind. Some time back, he was involved with Chōshichi-san of the Kimikawa, and when she got sick and couldn't work for three years, he let her stay in his summer house and took care of her the whole time. At least that's what I've heard."

"Really? I suppose if he's that sort of man . . . he might be willing to overlook a few indiscretions. I want someone who'll look after me, who'll be patient and not get angry over every little thing, and at this point I don't care what he looks like."

"But you already have a handsome *danna* like Yō-san—how can the rest of us keep up?"

"Is Yō-san really all that handsome? He reminds me of the man in that advertisement for Jintan pills. We're together because of our past, but I don't think he's particularly good-looking. And you know, Hana-chan, I don't think it's going to last."

"Why? Have you found someone else?"

"No, it's not that, but there's the matter of buying my contract, and then . . ." Komayo's voice trailed off and she looked down at her lap. In fact, she had met Segawa again last night at the Gishun, and their intimacy had grown to the point that she now realized she wouldn't be able to hide it from Yoshioka much longer. If he were any other customer, she might have been able to fool him, but Yoshioka was no ordinary patron. She had been his geisha, and she knew better than anyone how discerning he could be. So Komayo had made up her mind: after enlisting Hanasuke as an ally, she would arrange her uncertain fortunes so that no one, neither her customers on the outside nor her colleagues in the house—including Jūkichi—could put up any obstacles to her love affair.

"Hana-chan, I could use a good chat. If you're free, why don't we go have dinner at the Ingōya or somewhere? The truth is, I can't decide what to do."

"Oh? Well, I don't have anything planned for tonight."

"Good! Then let's go." Komayo leapt to her feet and called the attendant. "Osada-san! We're going to the Ingōya. There may be a call from the Gishun between seven and eight o'clock. We should be back by then, but if they phone, please let me know."

The two women came fluttering down the stairs.

As they did so, the elderly Gozan, watering can in hand, made his way up to tend to the morning glories that grew on the platform beneath the drying rack. He stepped out onto the roof at just the moment when shamisen practice in the neighboring houses fell silent, giving way to the hour of the bath, when cotton robes hung out to dry flapped in the evening breeze carrying the smell of coal fires and telephones began to ring impatiently. Evening in the pleasure quarters. There on the platform, he stood admiring the beauty of the scalloped clouds that covered the sky. Forgetting to count the buds on his plants, he watched the crows as they flew home toward the woods that surrounded the Hama Palace.

8. Crimes in Bed

Komayo had just returned with Hanasuke from the Ingōya and was having a smoke when she received the call she'd been hoping for. As soon as she arrived at the Gishun, she sent word for Hanasuke to join them, in order to introduce her to Segawa nii-san, and the three of them amused themselves until past ten o'clock when Hanasuke moved on to another

engagement. At this point, Komayo and Segawa retired to an inner room, intending to stay only until midnight. But they were
young and full of new passion, and when the time came, they
found it too difficult to part. The prospect of spending the night
together seemed all the more appealing, since Segawa had no
rehearsals scheduled for the next day.

They woke much later from a nap filled with pleasant dreams
and had a bath to wash away the sweat of a night and day together. Then, even though they'd had nothing to eat, they sat down
for a cup of saké just as the maid came in.

"Komayo-san, the telephone . . . ," she murmured, her voice
full of regret at having to disturb them.

Komayo went down to ask where the call had come from, but
when the attendant told her it was from a *machiai* known as the
Taigetsu, she asked to be excused. Returning to their room, she
curled up at Segawa's knees. They were sharing a bowl of soup
and some sweetfish grilled in salt when the maid reappeared to
summon her again to the phone.

"Nii-san, I want to go away with you," Komayo said, "somewhere far from here." But even as she spoke, she knew that this
was her job and nothing could be done about it. She went back
to the phone, and this time it was Hanasuke. Someone wanted
to see her, so would she please come if only for a few minutes?
They were waiting for her at the Taigetsu.

Komayo agreed reluctantly but asked Segawa to stay, promising she'd be back in an hour. Still hesitant, she took a *rikisha*
home to quickly repair her makeup and hair before going on to
the Taigetsu.

A single client was waiting for her in a large, airy room on
the upper floor of the *machiai*; but the surrounding party was
quite lively, with two senior geisha—their own Jūkichi and a
slightly younger woman named Fusahachi—several women
in their early twenties, including Hanasuke, Ineka, Hagiha,
Kineko, and Oboro, and two apprentices all in attendance. Komayo was secretly delighted to see so many women, thinking

she would have no problem escaping after a short stay. Yet it would never do to behave so selfishly with Jūkichi at hand—or so she was thinking when the latter abruptly got up to go to another engagement, politely promising to see their host again in the near future.

The client was an enormous, swarthy man in his fifties, fat and round as the sea monster known as the Umibōzu. He had taken off his jacket. His dark blue kimono was decorated with splashes of white and tied up with a stiff obi. He wore a signet ring on his little finger, like the regulars at the stock exchange in Kabuto-chō. The senior geisha, Fusahachi, was seated on one side of him with Hanasuke on the other, and both were pouring him beer. He seemed to have little to say but sat with a smirk on his face, listening with apparent interest as Kineko, Hagiha, and Ineka—women in their sexual prime—boasted of their amorous adventures or the apprentices offered their unschooled opinions of the current crop of child actors.

Seeing an opportunity to escape, Komayo got up quietly to go down to the office below; but she was stopped in the hallway by Hanasuke, who had also slipped from the room.

"Komayo," she called and then lowered her voice. "Are you free tonight?" At Komayo's puzzled look, Hanasuke drew closer. "You see, after I left the Gishun last night, I had an engagement with this man. He was very anxious to have you come, but it was late and I knew you were with Segawa-san, so I made up an excuse. But now, here he is again tonight and he wants me to arrange things with you. He's a big antique dealer from Yokohama. He used to have a shop in Nihonbashi, and I would see him from time to time in Yoshi-chō. We've met a few times since I came to Shimbashi, but he doesn't seem to have a regular girl."

Step by step, Hanasuke had pushed her down the hall to an empty room at the corner, and she seemed determined to have the matter decided on the spot. Komayo stood frozen for a moment, at a loss for an answer. It was unthinkable that she should give in to such a request from a client she'd met for the first time tonight. Yet it also was impossible to tell Hanasuke suddenly that everything she'd said over their steak dinner the evening before, her heartfelt confession and her plea for help in securing another patron, had all been a lie.

"Koma-chan, you'd have nothing to worry about with him, even if he found out about Segawa-san. He always says that he wouldn't even bother keeping a geisha who wasn't interested in having an actor on the side. He loves to show off, and not even one of those petty cabinet ministers or an aristocrat would ever be as generous. I know I may have spoken out of turn, but I was afraid someone else would get hold of him—so last night I told him about you and asked him to look after you."

Komayo let out a cry of dismay. Her face turned bright red and tears welled up in her eyes, but Hanasuke seemed to notice nothing in the dim light coming from the corridor. While Hanasuke was certainly accommodating, she also was careless and tended to jump to conclusions, so it was entirely possible that she mistook Komayo's cry for an exclamation of surprise at her unexpected good luck and interpreted her squirming and apparent reluctance as nothing more than a passing disappointment at the sudden appearance of a customer when she'd been looking forward to spending the night with Segawa. As a woman herself, Hanasuke found her reaction completely natural, but she also felt that such unfortunate developments were unavoidable in their profession. If one were willing to put up with the "unavoidable," it would soon bear its own fruit—a thought that came to her out of the unstinting kindness common in women who lead unvirtuous lives. What's more, if by fair means or foul she could procure Komayo tonight, the *machiai* would be left out of the calculation, and she would be able to keep a portion of the customer's tip. Twenty yen if he left fifty, fifty yen if he left one hundred. This was a tidy sum for a plain geisha from the humbler ranks such as Hanasuke, especially for one who was so acquisitive, who never left the house without her savings book. She had no intention of waiting for a reply from Komayo, sensing that if she did, what was possible might become impossible in the meantime. She only had to drive Komayo into a corner and the rest would take care of itself, and knowing from experience how things were likely to develop, she took the initiative.

"So then I'm counting on you. Good luck." Leaving Komayo standing in the empty room, she slipped out and hurried toward the stairs, not even giving her time to demur. Komayo's heart was pounding in her chest and she felt dazed, but she couldn't stand there forever. Just at that moment, in fact, she heard footsteps in the corridor—no doubt one of the maids—and, unable to think of anything else to do, she went back to the party. She noticed that Fusahachi, the old geisha, already was gone, and then almost immediately the others started taking their leave one by one: Ineka, Oboro, Kineko, and Hagiha. Finally, she was left alone with the apprentice, Tobimaru, and the antique dealer who looked now even more like a sea monster. He was still calmly drinking his saké while one of the maids fanned his back.

Komayo was appalled at the speed with which everything had unfolded, but she could say nothing, caught as she was between the urge to break down in tears and her pathetic resolve to drink this bitter cup to its dregs.

The Taigetsu *machiai* not only owned the Sanshun'en villa in Morigasaki but also was known to have the most beautiful garden of all the teahouses in Shimbashi. In the center was a rock-studded pond that reflected the light of the stone lanterns, and at the very back, shielded from view by a low fence and thick undergrowth, was a pavilion—to which, according to plan, Komayo and her client, shod in garden slippers, now at last made their way.

Opening the paper doors, they found a small room of just three tatami mats with a toilet at the end of the veranda. From the oblong brazier made of paulownia wood and the mulberry dresser to the lacquer kimono stand, everything was carefully arranged so that the occupants could manage without calling a maid. Beyond a high screen of wood and reed, the inner room seemed larger, visible in the half light of a small lamp shaded in silk. The mosquito net that hung in the room was made of fine, seamless gauze dyed a cool water green along the hem. The linen coverlet of the futon inside it was decorated with a scene filled with chrysanthemums. It had been turned back, revealing a mattress dyed in a bush clover pattern of pale blue and a long pillow edged with crimson tassels. Next to the bed was a tobacco pouch in the shape of a crescent and a carafe of water with glasses. A wind chime whispered quietly of the pleasures of the midautumn night that had descended over the city, bringing a profound sense of peace. The sea monster was silent, his eyes, dim with saké, passing back and forth between the enticing scene of the bed and the melancholy figure of the woman seated with her back to the lamp. Like a gourmet before an array of delicacies, he seemed unsure where to begin; but he was in no hurry, choosing instead to study the prospects carefully, determined, when the time came, to lick the carcass down to the marrow, according to some private design of his own. For her part, Komayo recoiled from those piercing eyes, and yet she knew there was no use objecting at this point. As long as she was in no real danger, no matter what happened she would simply close her eyes and try to bring things to a conclusion as quickly as possible. Her only thought was for Segawa, who was waiting for her at the Gishun, and how she could escape to join him sooner. Finally, unable to wait any longer, she spoke up in a voice tinged with nervousness and impatience.

"Dear . . . ," she said, leaning toward him invitingly. In that hoarse tone peculiar to rich, fat old men, he tried to respond, but something seemed to get in the way and he let out an enormous cough instead. Then, as if the cough had been a signal, he grabbed her hips, still wrapped in the obi, pulled her quickly onto his lap, and embraced her with enormous strength. She let out a muffled cry and closed her eyes as his fetid breath burned her cheek. Clenching her teeth, she managed to free her hands and cover her face.

A night of pleasure seems to pass in a moment, but a moment

of pain lasts an age. When Komayo finally escaped the pavilion, she glanced around the garden anxiously before making her way to the office to call for a *rikisha*. She found Hanasuke there smoking and daydreaming, apparently waiting for a *rikisha* herself, and it occurred to Komayo to wonder whether the whole thing had taken far less time than she'd imagined. At the sight of Hanasuke she felt a surge of shame and regret, and if she hadn't been in the office of a *machiai*, she would have liked to lash out at her. Hanasuke, however, behaved as though nothing had happened.

"They're looking for you at the house. O-Sada was just here. She said she'd call again later."

"Fine!"

Komayo had to speak with the attendant in order to call a *rikisha*, but when she reached O-Sada on the phone, she was told that Yoshioka-san had been waiting for her for some time and she would have to stop by the Hamazaki. Why had everything gone wrong this evening? Had she known how difficult it was going to be, she never would have promised to meet Segawa later, but now there was nothing to be done. If it had been an ordinary engagement, she simply would have refused; but it was her patron, Yoshioka, who had called, and this for the first time since the misadventure at the Sanshun'en. She would have to go, even though she knew that once there she would not be able to leave before he did. But Segawa would be angry, waiting for her at the Gishun, and might even call another geisha out of pique. The thought was excruciating. Nevertheless, hiding away her feelings in her heart, she set off for the Hamazaki.

It was past nine o'clock. Since a car always came to take Yoshioka home at eleven, the obliging maid led Komayo directly to his room on the first floor. She was relieved to know when she would be free again but vexed all the same at the prospect of undoing the sash she had only just retied. At the sight of the futon already spread out in the room, she let out an involuntary sigh. Since the day before yesterday, night and day, she and Segawa had abandoned themselves to pleasure until her body was like a limp rag. Then she'd been taken forcibly by the monster at the Taigetsu, a man of such brutality that she was afraid of being injured. The ride in the *rikisha* on the way to the Hamazaki had been a brief respite. But now, before her pulse had even returned to normal, she would have to perform for her patron, whose habits she knew so well. Even under normal circumstances, she had secretly found his attentions excessive, but in her current state of exhaustion it was almost too much to contemplate. Nor could it be compared with the unpleasant surprise she'd just had at the Taigetsu: this time she knew exactly what to expect—for the next hour and a half, until eleven o'clock, she would be subjected to his ardor without a moment's rest, without even time for a cigarette. Worse still, she couldn't simply lie back and let him do as he liked. Yoshioka had convinced himself that he was the only man in her life and, since they weren't together every night, that she burned with longing for him—a longing he was determined to satisfy by means of an endless repertoire of indecent techniques. Komayo had been a geisha long enough to be able to endure these attentions, distasteful though she sometimes found them. But she was a flesh-and-blood woman, and in spite of herself she realized that she responded to him and wanted to convince him of her good faith. It would never do to give away her affair with Segawa by an abrupt change in the way she treated her *danna*, particularly since Yoshioka seemed to be so sensitive to this sort of thing. If she didn't take the initiative, didn't appear to seduce him, then she was sure he would immediately become suspicious. Moreover, this was their first meeting since leaving the Sanshun'en, and she still had not answered his proposal to repay her debt; she would have to be even more ardent than usual to allay his suspicions and assure him of her loyalty. The more she thought about it, the more pitiful and sad she felt. She wanted to put her hands together and beg him to leave her alone, just this one night. But Yoshioka would proceed as always as if nothing had happened, calmly, deliberately, taking full advantage of his considerable prowess and long experience, which had prevailed over so many women, from girls of sixteen to women past forty. He would conduct his experiments, trying one thing and then another, until he was completely satisfied with the results, as though his very honor depended on it.

At eleven o'clock, when he finally released her, she was breathless and almost unable to rise from the bed. Clearly pleased to see her in such a state, Yoshioka called for his car and disappeared into the darkness. Komayo had barely managed to see him off at the gate, but once she had made her way back to the office of the Hamazaki, she found she no longer wanted to go on to the Gishun or go home. Her only thought was to find a deserted spot—an empty house, a barren field—a place to abandon her worn-out body. Even if she had wanted to go to Segawa, how could she when she'd been used by two men in the same night? Nor was she capable of giving herself to him without telling him what had happened, to show she wasn't to blame. It had all been in the line of duty, of course; but when she recalled the events of the evening, she felt a vivid shame and moved away from the light in the office to avoid prying eyes. If she were to find herself in front of her makeup stand just now, she had a feeling that the more white powder she applied, the dirtier her face would look, that the more she combed her hair, the more disheveled it would become.

As she stood there lost in thought, she heard a voice calling from outside the lattice door.

"I've come for Komayo-san." It was the *rikisha* driver.

"Thank you," she said, climbing into the seat. He asked where she wanted to go. "To the Gishun," she said, and before she had time to change her mind, the driver had set off. Closing her eyes and pressing the amulet she carried tucked in her obi, she muttered a prayer for Segawa's forgiveness, reminding herself that everything she had done had been for him.

Just as she'd imagined, she found Segawa sleeping alone. It seemed that he had been waiting for her, since he lay on half the futon with a second pillow next to his own. His arm was stretched out, as if to invite her to rest her head on it without further delay. Komayo was delighted by his thoughtfulness, but it made her realize how exhausted she was. The sigh that escaped her lips spoke of her ordeal with Yoshioka and the customer at the Taigetsu. Weary to the bone and yet outraged at having been toyed with by these other men, she suddenly fell on Segawa as if in vengeance, embracing him with a passion that was almost masculine. Startled, he woke to find her crying, her face pressed against his.

9. *The Autumn Review*

Twice a year, in spring and autumn, the geisha of Shimbashi gave a three-day performance at the Kabukiza. The time for the autumn review had finally come, and the curtain had just fallen on the opening piece, a grand dance by all the artists in the quarter.

"I'm glad we came early. 'The Lake of Otama' comes just after this next number." The woman who had spoken was about thirty-five and wore her hair in the rounded *marumage* style of married women. From the way she handed him her program and busied herself pouring tea, it was clear that she was the wife of the writer Kurayama Nansō. Next to her was a charming, bright-eyed girl of twelve or thirteen, obviously her daughter, and a woman of perhaps fifty, also in compact *marumage*, who wore a finely patterned *haori* jacket decorated with the crest of the Uji school of singing and dancing. She seemed to be their music teacher. The party occupied a box slightly to the right of center.

"Oh, thank you," said the teacher, taking a cup of tea. "It must be nearly ten years since they performed this *jōruri* play of yours," she said, turning to Nansō. "It was the previous Segawa who did it if I'm not mistaken."

"That's right. I'm not sure why, but they've been reviving my worthless old plays these past few years. To tell the truth, it makes me a bit uncomfortable."

"He always complains when they perform one of his plays," said Nansō's wife. "But, I say, if it bothers him so much, he'd have been better off never writing them to begin with." Laughing merrily, she began slicing a bar of sweet bean-paste for her daughter.

Nansō laughed as well as he glanced down at the program. The third number was one of his old ballads in the *jōruri* style, something called "The Lake of Otama: A True Chronicle," and the program listed the Tokizawa musicians who would play the accompaniment and the three geisha who were to dance. But Nansō soon looked up again, much more interested in the crowds filling the theater around him. The latecomers were pressing in, and the corridors and the passages between the two *hanamichi* runways were full of people coming and going or greeting friends in the crush.

Rather than watch a performance of one of his plays, Nansō much preferred to let his eyes wander across the theater, examining the crowd, the gawkers, the current fashion in clothes and hairstyles, and the like. Thus, whenever he received an invitation to the theater as either a critic or a playwright, he made a point of attending, regardless of whether it took him to the most obscure playhouse or a great stage like this one. These days, however, he no longer engaged in the passionate debates that had consumed him ten years ago. In fact, even when the play itself was worthless, he made an effort to write a pleasant, favorable review—although at times, despite his good intentions, the compliments had a way of revealing his natural irony. This, in turn, delighted the more knowledgeable theatergoers. So even though Nansō himself set little store by them, his reviews were unusually influential in unexpected quarters. Ten years ago, when he'd been an avid theatergoer himself, he had made a concerted effort to create new kabuki plays in the traditional style. But as the years passed, tastes had changed. New styles in staging and acting had developed, and the likes and dislikes of the audience had shifted—usually in a direction that was quite the opposite from his own perspective. This, however, was the way of the world, and rather than become upset and rail against the new order, he had simply distanced himself from the theater. Recently, though, by some inexplicable accident of fashion, theaters had begun reviving his old plays once or twice a year. At first, he found this rather disconcerting; then he had a change of heart, taking a secret pleasure in the thought that the philistines had finally seen the light. But in the end he realized that the public had an insatiable appetite for everything without distinction, the good and the bad, the new and the old, and he decided it all was just a matter of chance. So now when he went to see one of his old plays, he simply surrendered to the memories of an earlier time that it evoked, in which joy and sorrow were strangely intermingled. In short, although he had allowed himself a whiff of greasepaint, he did not let it go to his head and rekindle old ambitions. Nansō had long since concluded that in all things he preferred the blur of memory to the hard focus of the present.

"Okine-san," he said, addressing himself to the music teacher. "Isn't that O-Man from the Ogie shamisen school, there in the second box on the east side? She's aged, hasn't she?"

"O-Man? Is she here? Madam, could you lend me the opera glasses for a moment? . . . You're right, it is O-Man. I never would have recognized her. And that's the mistress of the Taigetsu in the box in front of her."

"She wasn't so large in the days when my father was a regular there, but I suppose that's what comes of success. She's turned into a regular sumo wrestler."

They watched small groups of geisha make their way to the boxes to pay their respects to the mistresses of the important houses in the quarter. The actors and other entertainers and assorted hangers-on all bowed low as they passed. Nansō found the constant stream of fruit, sushi, and other gifts being delivered to the boxes far more interesting to watch than anything that was happening on stage. In fact, the audience today was quite different from the usual theater crowd. Every box, east and west, was filled with the women who ran the principal *machiai* and their geisha, primarily from Shimbashi but from other quarters throughout the city as well, women who had come out of a sense of obligation to their Shimbashi sisters. Then there were the actors and their wives, masters and teachers from the various music schools, sumo wrestlers, and professional flatterers of all sorts. Visible in the midst of this crowd and commanding its attention and respect, were assorted gentlemen, patrons, and highly placed officials, as well as men of the opposite sort, the parasites of the demimonde, hanging about in their dark serge *hakama* or in Western dress. Finally, gathered at the back of the lowest level, were the geisha-house proprietors, the maids and attendants, friends and relatives.

Nansō had gone out into the corridor to wander about and watch the comings and goings when suddenly he heard a cheerful greeting.

"Sensei, how good of you to come!" Turning to look, he found Komayo of the Obanaya standing there. She was wearing a dark kimono with a white underrobe and a pattern dyed at the hem. Her hair was done up in an old style favored by dancers.

"What piece are you performing?" Nansō asked.

"I'm dancing 'Yasuna.'"

"And when are you on?"

"Not for a while yet. I'm fifth, I think."

"The perfect position. Not too early or too late, just as the audience is paying closest attention."

"Oh dear! Now I'm even more nervous."

"And how is Gozan?"

"Quite well, thank you. He should be here soon. He said that he'd come with Jūkichi."

A geisha, her hair done in the same style, passed them in the corridor. "The dance teacher was looking for you just now," she said, glancing back at Komayo.

"Really? Then I should be going. Sensei, I hope you enjoy the performance." So saying, she turned and hurried off through the crowd. At that moment, the wooden clappers announced the start of the next number on the stage, and the press in the hall became even more frenzied; but not a soul, man or woman, failed to turn to watch Komayo as she passed. The attention made her feel a bit uneasy, though she also was elated. At the time of the spring performances, she had only just come back to the quarter and had no one to help her with the expense of taking a leading role. On the advice of her teacher, she had agreed to join another geisha who was performing "The Monkey Trainer," and she'd been forced to take the minor part of O-Some. Fortunately, the performance had been very well received, and for some time afterward she was kept busy with calls from parties wanting her to dance. The experience had given her a great deal of confidence and had left her determined to make much more of a splash in the autumn performance, one that would leave the audience with mouths agape. What's more, she no longer had to worry about the expense, with both Yoshioka-san and the new patron, whose existence she'd kept hidden, equally willing to assist her. As for artistic matters, she had the support of a professional, Segawa Isshi, who had taught her the tricks of his trade and had promised to lend her his attendants on the day itself. All in all, she felt as though she'd already become a famous performer. If her piece today were to get even better reviews than her last effort did, she would immediately be known as the star of Shimbashi dance, and her reputation as a geisha of the first rank would be known to all. She could only hope that everything would go according to plan, even though she knew she would be a bundle of nerves until the curtain opened.

Passing through a door at the end of the hall, she made her way behind the stage and hurried to a room on the second floor that was usually reserved for Segawa when kabuki was being performed. During the past three days she'd been given the use of his room, and it filled her with secret delight to apply her makeup in front of his mirror and receive the special attentions of his assistants and minions. It was almost more than she could put into words.

Segawa was already in the dressing room, apparently having used the stage door to pay her a visit. He was just removing his coat of fine serge wool when Komayo made a hurried entrance.

"After all those calls to make sure I wouldn't be late, you're just arriving?"

"I'm so sorry," she said, sitting close beside him despite the presence of his attendants. "I've been out front paying my respects. But I want to thank you from the bottom of my heart for everything you've done."

"No speeches now. Is there still time before your number?"

"Yes, plenty."

"And is there anyone important out front?"

"Of course," she said, mentioning the names of several well-known actors. "They're all here."

"Really?"

"They've all come *with* someone." Without quite knowing why, Komayo had laid extra stress on the words, but she realized immediately what she'd done. "You don't suppose I'm jealous?" she added with a laugh.

Just then, the hairdresser entered with Komayo's wig.

10. *Box Seat*

Yoshioka and his colleague Eda took their seats in a lower-tier box on the east side of the theater shortly before Komayo was to perform "Yasuna." They were joined by the mistress of the Hamazaki, along with Hanasuke and the apprentice

Hanako from Komayo's house. As it happened, Yoshioka was furious when Komayo refused his offer to buy her contract at the end of summer and considered breaking off with her. But for the time being he could find no one to replace her, and despite his anger, he was at a loss as to how to conclude the affair. So in the end he found himself accepting the various apologies offered on Komayo's behalf by the mistress of the Hamazaki—a woman skilled in such matters—and he had agreed to go on supporting her as before. Still, their meetings had become much less frequent. He and Eda would show up once every ten days or so, just for a drink, as if he had decided that he would be able to save face as a proper patron simply by fulfilling the minimum duties. As a result, he had no idea that Komayo was carrying on an affair with Segawa nor that she had found a second patron as well.

Long years of constant indulgence in the pleasures of the geisha had left Yoshioka somewhat jaded; and ever since the day they left the Sanshun'en, he had been leading a rather quiet, mundane existence. He went straight home from work and went to bed early. On Sundays and holidays, he would take his wife and children to the zoo or some other entertainment. He did not find this new life particularly lonely or boring, nor was it especially interesting or amusing; the days simply passed in a vague blur. But now for the first time in quite a while, he found himself seated in a box at the Kabukiza looking out over a room filled with chattering beauties, and he felt as though he had suddenly awakened from a long sleep. The desire to taste the various pleasures that the world had to offer was stirring in him again. Yoshioka's need to experience the carnal delights of civilized society was not unlike the urge that in ancient times led men to mount their steeds and chase wild beasts across the plains, to kill them and eat their flesh; the same urge that led medieval warriors to don fine armor and shed their blood on the field of combat. They all were simply manifestations of that pathetic, and yet seemingly limitless, human energy known as desire. With the advance of civilization, this energy was trans-

formed, expressing itself now as the pursuit of luxury and pleasure, or else as the will to dominate in the business world. Fame,
wealth, and women—these were the driving forces in the life
of the modern man. Anyone who disdained or despised them,
anyone who feared them, was simply a coward who lacked the
courage for the fight or a failure who already had lost it. As these
thoughts ran through his mind, Yoshioka realized that the scene
here in the theater had, to some degree, restored his will to be
more active while reassuring him that he was still young enough
to do so.

The clappers sounded again, and at last the curtains parted for
Komayo's dance. The Kiyomoto chanters began to sing the words
to the ballad, and applause could be heard here and there in the
hall. Three apprentice geisha hurried by Yoshioka's box on the
way back to their seats.

"Look, it's 'Yasuna,'" said one.

"Komayo-san's dancing—it should be wonderful."

"Of course," said the third. "She's got Segawa-san to help her."

"They say they're quite serious."

Amid the surrounding hubbub, by some strange chance
these voices came through clearly to Yoshioka. He turned instinctively toward them, but the three apprentices already were
disappearing in the crowd, leaving behind only a glimpse of
their knotted sashes and the patterns on their long sleeves.
He had no idea who they were or to which house they might
belong.

But the last phrase—"They say they're quite serious"—had
been more than enough. If the words had been said straight to
his face and out of some sort of malice, there might have been
room for doubt. But coming so naturally from the mouth of
an innocent apprentice, in the form of gossip overheard from
someone who did not know he was listening—he had no choice
but to accept it as the truth. Could there be a clearer example of
the old saying "With no mouths of their own, the gods speak
through the mouths of men"? Having reached this conclusion,

Yoshioka thought back over Komayo's behavior since their falling out, reviewing her actions in minute detail. At the same time, it occurred to him to wonder whether Eda, who had been with him almost constantly, had already learned of the affair. If he had, was he keeping quiet out of pity? Under the circumstances, Yoshioka would certainly have preferred to have been the first to get wind of this. To have others know sooner would suggest he was naive or distracted, quite the opposite of the image of the seasoned connoisseur he had cultivated for so long in the quarter. The more deeply he felt the shame of it, the more furious he became with Komayo.

Seated on the platform to the right of the stage, the musicians chanted in unison:

> Like water breaking on a rock,
> Tears of unrequited love
> Flow on my breast.

The prologue of the ballad ended, and in the silence that followed, the first beats of the hand drums called attention to Yasuna's long-awaited entrance. Every eye in the audience turned to watch the curtains part at the back of the theater. From there, Komayo would make her way to the stage along the *hanamichi* runway. Up in the balcony, people already were applauding. But in his anger, Yoshioka couldn't bear to watch her in the role of the grief-mad lover, dragging his dead lady's gown through grasses heavy with the morning dew. He turned away, making a show of looking up at the broad ceiling, and began thinking back over the various excuses Komayo had made when he offered to pay her debt and take her as his mistress. However distasteful, he would have to give the problem serious consideration. Until today, he had never understood the things she'd said to him, but now suddenly everything became clear. The time had come to be rid of the woman, but he wanted to outwit her, to beat her at her own game while pretending to know nothing about it. Of course, it would never do to simply go back to Rikiji. But out of the hundreds of geisha in Shimbashi, surely there must be one he could choose who would make Komayo suffer. His eyes roamed over every geisha in sight, from the orchestra to the boxes to the women standing in the aisles. All the faces in the audience were turned toward the stage where Komayo's Yasuna had begun the frantic search for his lost love. Just at that moment, the door to Yoshioka's box opened and a voice whispered a greeting.

"I'm sorry to be so late." It was Kikuchiyo of the Obanaya, the woman whose makeup was so thick that her crueler sisters were not above noting her resemblance to a whore. She had sung a supporting role in "Kairaishi," the second number on the program, so her hair was still done in a swept-up *shimada* style and her elaborate kimono was embroidered with gold thread from the hem to the collar. Yoshioka turned at the sound of the door opening, and in the dim light her face, even more heavily larded than usual, reminded him of the stuffed rag figures that decorate a New Year's battledore. To other women, Kikuchiyo's ill-assorted features were no doubt unattractive. But a man's eyes were drawn first to her tempting, malleable flesh, which, like her makeup, seemed to be layered thickly over her whole body. If her manners and comportment were somehow lacking or even a little crude, there were times when that could be more desirable, more stimulating than the refined charms of her more accomplished sisters.

Since she had arrived late and the box was already full, Kikuchiyo was forced to sit in the middle of the group, practically in Yoshioka's lap. The collar of her kimono was pulled back seductively, and from this vantage point, he could study the voluptuous, snow white flesh on her neck; and looking down, he could see the bleached crepe collar of her undergown peaking out from the heavy white taffeta collar of her underkimono. He thought perhaps he had even caught a trace of that warm, inimitable scent given off by a woman's bare body.

Yoshioka recalled that there was a rivalry between Kikuchiyo and Komayo that erupted at the slightest provocation. There were hints of it even in today's performance. Since Komayo had chosen to dance "Yasuna," a piece from the repertoire of the Kiyomoto school in which Kikuchiyo had trained, it would have been only natural to have asked a sister geisha from her house to be part of the accompaniment. But no doubt out of concern that this would detract from the performance, she had asked Segawa Isshi to procure some professional accompanists and had willingly paid an enormous sum for their services. Nor was it a question of finding Kikuchiyo's singing unpleasant or her talents deficient. For Komayo, the only thing that mattered was making her dance stand out from the others. Obsessed with the idea of proving, with this one performance, that she was the finest dancer in Shimbashi, she'd had no time to consider other aspects of the matter.

But for Kikuchiyo, this all had been most unpleasant, and she had no desire to be sitting in this box, of all places, watching Komayo's triumph. Still, recognizing her obligations to an important patron of the teahouses, she had come to pay her respects and convey the obligatory compliments to Komayo's *danna*— even though all the while, inside, she was so livid and miserable she wanted to weep.

> Deceived by crows we thought announced the dawn,
> I make my way alone,
> Regretting the end of our night of love,
> Love that might have gone on
> And on till morning.

The dance was reaching its climax. The mistress of the Hamazaki and Hanasuke were busy directing flattery at Komayo's patron.

"She's become a real artist, hasn't she?"

"Practice makes all the difference."

"She's utterly flawless."

Listening to this praise for her rival, Kikuchiyo could only suffer, taking shallow breaths. But Yoshioka's rage had risen to a frenzy now, and in his need to punish Komayo, he felt a violent urge to take this other woman in her stead. As the dance reached the passage known as "Within the curtains, curtains of leaves," he grasped Kikuchiyo's hand and held it tight.

Kikuchiyo sat quietly, making no attempt to pull free. She seemed intent on pretending that nothing had happened, but unsure where to look, she gazed vaguely in the direction of the stage. Yoshioka watched for a sign of her reaction, keeping hold of her hand until their palms were damp with sweat. Having abandoned one hand to him, Kikuchiyo seemed to be using the other to search for a cigarette. Without a word, he took the gold-tipped Mikasa he was smoking and passed it to her. It amused him to see how calmly she took it and placed it between her lips. Determined to force the issue, he craned his neck forward as if to get a better view of the stage. This position left him free to press his cheek against hers while rubbing his knee on her back.

Even then, she sat quietly, giving no sign that she objected. Realizing at last that she must have understood his intentions, Yoshioka was deeply satisfied. His vanity as a *danna* led him to assume that she had secretly been infatuated with him for some time. No doubt she'd observed how solicitous he was with Komayo and had long wanted such a patron for her own. If that were the case, then this was going to be more amusing than he'd imagined—or so he told himself as he went about dissecting the woman's feelings in his head.

Kikuchiyo was not an authentic Shimbashi geisha trained in the traditional manner. Born the daughter of a shopkeeper in the western quarters of the city, at fifteen she had been sent into service as a lady's maid in the household of a certain viscount who was then a minister in the government. Even before the tucks had been taken from the shoulders of her kimono, marking her passage into womanhood, she became involved in a relationship with a young student who also was in service at the house. Soon she found herself submitting to the viscount as well, and for a time she shuttled back and forth between master and servant, old man and youth. At some point, however, the viscount's son returned from his studies abroad, and she also took up with him. Finally the old man began wondering how he could extricate himself from these potentially embarrassing circumstances. Fortunately, at about this same time, Jūkichi, a geisha with whom he'd had dealings for some years, came to pay her traditional midsummer greetings. When the viscount laid the problem out for her, Jūkichi immediately proposed that the girl become a geisha. If she already showed such tendencies, then she certainly had a promising future in the profession. For her part, the girl had always wanted to be a geisha, attracted as she was to the fine kimono they wore to their banquets and garden parties. So matters were easily arranged, although to preserve appearances the girl was required to leave the household and return home for a period before passing into Jūkichi's care and making her debut as Kikuchiyo of the Obanaya. She was eighteen at the time and white and plump as a rubber doll— just the thing to delight gentlemen of a certain age—and she soon found herself quite busy with engagements. Nor did she mind when she was sent out to clients whom the other geisha found too difficult. Somehow Kikuchiyo alone managed to satisfy them. Raised as they had been in the old school, Jūkichi and her husband Gozan were surprised by the universal praise the girl received from the proprietors of the quarter's teahouses, and they could only marvel at the audacity of this new sort of woman. But in other matters, such as her general comportment at an engagement or her way of greeting senior geisha, she was impossible to train—so much so that Gozan, always a stickler for protocol, once even suggested that she be sent elsewhere for fear that the presence of such a loose woman might damage the reputation of their house. In the end, however, there was no denying that she was popular, and so despite the difficulties and embarrassments, she stayed on. In addition to all her other duties, Jūkichi took on the task of trying to train her in the fundamentals of the performing arts. It was thanks to this attention, no doubt, that in a year or two she finally seemed to understand the principles of her profession, had found herself two or three regular patrons, and had become the geisha she was today: a woman able to sing the supporting role in "Kairishi" at the Kabukiza.

Kikuchiyo had none of the pride and willfulness of a woman like Komayo, who had been trained as a geisha almost from birth. By contrast, Kikuchiyo was completely indiscriminate, making no distinction at all between a doddering old man and one hardly wet behind the ears, between the rustic and the dandy. For her, all clients—for that matter, all men—were alike: once they'd had enough to drink, they became animals. It was not a conclusion she'd reached consciously; she simply had always felt this to be the case. She did not find this especially shameful or repugnant, nor did she think it something admirable. For all these reasons, however, she seemed to have little trouble putting up with things that less robust women found quite insufferable. There even were rumors that she occasionally initiated this sort of sport herself, leading to her reputation in the quarter as a woman of questionable morals.

These rumors, of course, only succeeded in exciting masculine curiosity, and Yoshioka, who had known of them for some time, often thought he would like to put them to the test had Kikuchiyo not been at the same house as Komayo. But now that he'd found the one person who could help him achieve his goal of humiliating Komayo, there was nothing to stop him from satisfying his curiosity. Suddenly, he was unable to wait until the program came to an end. The music of "Yasuna" returned to its basic motif.

> Is there someone who resembles her? Tell me!
> Her form, her kimono. I fear for my sanity!

As the wooden clapper echoed through the hall, Yoshioka, almost beside himself, got quickly to his feet.

11. *The Kikuobana*

It was the day after the dance recital had finished
its successful three-day run, and it was quiet in the Shimbashi
quarter. The sounds of shamisen practice, which could be heard
in every house all year-round from early each morning, were suddenly stilled. The usual stream of women going back and forth to
music and dance lessons had grown so sparse that from Kompa-
ru-dōri through Naka-dōri and Itajinmichi to Shigarakijinmichi
on the far side, the streets seemed quiet and weary, as they do the
day after a festival. From time to time, a teahouse attendant or a
group of three or four well-known senior geisha could be seen
hurrying by. To the casual observer, it might have seemed they
were simply putting things in order again after the performance.
But the younger geisha were alert to their movements, knowing
that they could provide clues to any new trouble or grievance that
had arisen in the quarter.

Grievances and discord were common enough among these
women. But a geisha would never stoop to the wily politician's
trick of stirring up trouble just to gain some advantage. Perhaps
geisha have more dignity than politicians do. Still, this morning
at the public bath, at the hairdressers, in the second-floor parlors
of the houses where the women idled away the hours—in every
place that geisha congregated—their usual jealous critiques of
one another's talents were mixed with a good deal of gossip, slan-
der, and outright libel. In particular, today, a rumor had reached
the upper floor of Jūkichi's Obanaya that Kikuchiyo, who had always been known as "Miss Easy" or "The Chinese Goldfish," had
suddenly been bought off. The apprentice Hanako had returned
home and told Komayo the story she'd heard from the hairdresser,
that Kikuchiyo had appeared that evening, even before the whole

recital had ended, and had asked to have her hair done in the *marumage* style of a married woman. The rumor spread like wildfire to the houses on either side of the Obanaya and to the three across the way. Then as it fanned out across the quarter, speculation began about which client had taken her. It seemed that Kikuchiyo had finished her role as accompanist at the Kabukiza yesterday evening and, after stopping in to have her hair redone, had disappeared with someone. There had been no phone call from her since she'd left the house in the afternoon, and even the attendant, O-Sada, had no idea where she might be. Kikuchiyo was known to have at least four regular patrons. But if the others she kept secret were added in, along with the possibility that someone else might have appeared out of the blue, it was all but impossible to guess where she had gone. When she had an engagement, she would always spend the night away from the house or, as often as not, end up going off on a trip with a client. She slept at the Obanaya no more than one or two nights a month, and even then, according to the other women, she seemed to prefer not to—although it's possible this was an exaggeration on their part.

"You know how she is. I doubt he's Japanese. If it's not a Westerner, it's probably a Chinaman." On the second floor of the Obanaya, the discussion went on without reaching a conclusion. Finally, agreeing that it must be a Chinese, they wandered out, some to visit a shrine, some to the bath, and others to the hairdresser.

Taking advantage of her solitude, Komayo seated herself in front of her bureau and began to calculate the expenses she'd incurred from three days of performing "Yasuna" at the Kabukiza. First there were the fees for her dance teacher and the Kiyomoto musicians, then the tips for the stagehands and dressers at the theater, as well as the special payments to Segawa's trainees and assistants. She added it all up—what had already been paid for, the unpaid bills, and other debts she had seemingly incurred—and after checking to make sure that nothing had been left out, she came to a grand total of more than six hundred yen. When she finished her calculations, she lit a cigarette and sat staring vacantly at her account book. Then suddenly, as if she'd just recalled something, she put the book away in a drawer and went to the phone. Wanting to pay a visit to thank the mistress of the Hamazaki, she called to make sure she was at home and then sent the maid out to the Fūgestudō to buy a gift certificate to take as a present.

Three nights ago, on the first evening of the recital, Yoshioka should have stopped by the Hamazaki and called for her. Instead, he had made some excuse and had hurried out of the theater before her dance was finished. There must be some reason for such behavior, and Komayo immediately felt guilty about her affair with Segawa. Since then, she had become increasingly worried, but on the night in question Yoshioka's absence had allowed her to linger with Segawa. He had held her hand as he guided her through the program again, going over the strengths and weaknesses of her performance, and the pleasure this gave her made her forget all about phoning the Hamazaki. The second evening had been lost to the antique dealer from Yokohama at the Taigestu, and last night she'd had an unexpected call from Sugishima-san, the client from Dairen she'd had to forcibly reject last spring just after she'd resumed her career. This time, too, she had found it difficult to come up with an excuse that would allow her to get away. So despite her good intentions, she had put off her courtesy call until today.

The mistress of the Hamazaki insisted that Yoshioka-san had not seemed upset about anything. He had said something to Eda, and then he left as if he had some pressing business. "And as you know," she concluded, "Eda-san stayed for one more number and then left by himself."

Secretly relieved and reassured, Komayo went home and placed two sword-shaped bean cakes she'd bought on the fox-god altar on her dresser, praying with all her heart for the good fortune they promised to bring her.

That evening, she went out to her engagements and returned

without incident. There still was no sign of Kikuchiyo, who apparently was spending the night elsewhere. Nor had they heard from her by the next evening when the women started putting on their makeup, and the attendant O-Sada began to worry that she'd had an accident. There was no more talk of a secret transaction. Now it was rumored that she had bought her way out without permission or that she had simply run away. To be sure, on several previous occasions, Kikuchiyo had gone off with a client to Hakone or Ikaho or even as far as Kyoto without so much as a call to the Obanaya. Thus, it could not be said that Jūkichi was especially surprised. But she was worried that Kikuchiyo's careless behavior would have a bad influence on the other girls in the house, and she went about grumbling that something would have to be done. Then, just as she was saying how unlikely it seemed that such a girl would be bought off, Kikuchiyo herself appeared at the door. Her *marumage* had come loose. It threatened to tumble from her head, held in place by nothing more than a bright red hair band, but Kikuchiyo seemed unconcerned. The thick makeup that normally covered her face had peeled away in patches, and there were gray stains of hair oil on the back of her neck—suggesting that she had got out of bed and come just as she was, without a bath or so much as a thought for her appearance. The slovenly way she'd tied her kimono and the bits of reddish dirt clinging to her stockings completed the picture so perfectly that even someone as kind and generous as Jūkichi was taken aback. It was the same for geisha as it was for actors, she thought: if you didn't train them properly from birth, they weren't worth presenting to the public once they were grown— although at the moment she was too shocked to offer even the mildest scolding. For her part, though, Kikuchiyo seemed completely oblivious.

"Nee-san," she said, her tone almost buoyant, "I have something to discuss with you."

So the rumors that she'd been ransomed weren't just rumors. The thought shocked Jūkichi all the more. Casting another glance at her, she led Kikuchiyo to a room in the back where they could be alone.

Barely half an hour later, Kikuchiyo came upstairs. Her hair was still sagging and her kimono was still askew, but she marched up the steps as though returning home in triumph. As the other women busied themselves getting ready for the evening's engagements, she collapsed in the middle of the room.

"This is my last evening here," she said, as if talking to herself.

"Nee-san, are congratulations in order?" The apprentice Hanako began the questioning.

"Yes, and I'm very happy about it," Kikuchiyo said, apparently to no one in particular. "Hana-chan, you must come visit me as soon as I've found a house for myself."

At this, the others could no longer keep quiet.

"Kiku-chan, how lucky for you! I'm so glad! So are you quitting for good, or will you set up your own place?" Hanasuke spoke first.

"I'd be bored if I quit completely. I'll be opening a house."

"That's wonderful!" Komayo chimed in. "There's nothing better than working at your own place."

"Who is it?" Hanasuke asked, holding up her thumb as a sign for "men." "It's O-san, isn't it?" But Kikuchiyo merely laughed and shook her head like a naughty child.

"Then it's Ya-san," said Komayo. Kikuchiyo laughed again. "Who then? Kii-chan, you can tell us! We're your friends."

"It's too embarrassing," she said, laughing more deeply now.

"And you the proper lady!"

"Well, it's someone you all know. He has quite a reputation in the quarter, so you'll find out soon enough."

Komayo left at this point, summoned by a phone call from the teahouse where she was engaged. As she entered the attendant's room where the geisha waited before making their appearance at the party, she realized that the expense of dancing "Yasuna" had been well worthwhile. The other women immediately fell to praising her performance, telling her how wonderful she had been, how talented she was. Then at the banquet, when she danced "Urashima" for the fifteen or sixteen guests and twenty or more geisha of all ages and ranks, she was greeted with warm applause and pressed to perform "Shiokumi" as an encore. Soon after she'd finished, she hurried off to her next engagement.

Making her way to the Hamazaki, she found Yoshioka waiting for her there. He told her that he'd heard that her housemate, Kikuchiyo, had been set up in business for herself and that he wanted to give her something by way of congratulation.

"And you should do the same," he said, forcing a ten-yen note on her despite her protests. He drank less than usual and after an hour he left, explaining that he was very busy with work just at the moment.

But at least she had seen him, she thought. She had saved face with the teahouse, and the fears that had haunted her since the first night of the recital had been laid to rest. She happily sent on the present to Kikuchiyo.

In the meantime, Kikuchiyo had found in Itajinmichi a vacant house that suited her and had hung out a sign that read "Kikuo-bana," a name meant to indicate her debt to her former house, the Obanaya. Since she continued to go to the same hairdresser, Komayo saw her from time to time, and she seemed quite the same as before, prattling on about nothing in particular. Consequently, it was quite some time before Komayo realized that the man who had paid for Kikuchiyo's release was none other than her own patron, Yoshioka. In this, however, she was not alone; no one in Shimbashi knew the identity of Kikuchiyo's lover.

His desire to cause Komayo pain had led Yoshioka to use all his skills at deception. On that first night at the Kabukiza, he had made some excuse to Eda and had gone alone to a teahouse he knew in Nihombashi. After calling Kikuchiyo to join him there, he had then persuaded her to set out for Mukōjima by car. It was Saturday and the first time since his stay at the Sanshun'en that he had indulged in this sort of adventure. Kikuchiyo had put up some resistance at first, but once the alcohol began to take effect, she had lived up to—indeed, surpassed—her considerable reputation, to the extent that her immodesty had made him wonder if she'd ever heard of feminine scruples. Yoshioka, who usually was so precise about his schedule, found himself phoning home to make his excuses so that he could stay on with her. And indeed, it was in passing a whole night with her that he came to fully appreciate just how rare and surprising her qualities were.

As a connoisseur of the pleasure quarters, he'd known many geisha in his time, but he'd never met a woman like her. She was exactly like those occidental whores who would sit, quite nude, on a man's lap and pass the night brandishing a glass of champagne. To all intents and purposes, in fact, he decided she *was* more of a foreign woman than a Japanese one. A list of her attributes and capacities would have to start with the whiteness of her skin. There might be other Japanese women with white skin, but none of them had the bloom that gave her body its ineffable appeal. Then there was the flesh itself. Although the ignorant might have called it pasty or doughy, in reality it was a perfect texture, neither too firm nor too soft, and so exquisitely smooth that the man who embraced her found himself melting completely into her. She was nicely ample even in places that were ordinarily lean—her throat and shoulders and flanks—but since her body itself was small and in constant, dizzying motion, she had none of the painful heaviness of a fat woman. His arms could hold her with ease, and she was as light as a feather on his lap. And when she was positioned over him, her breasts wriggled delightfully against his chest. Her buttocks, firm as rubber balls, fitted perfectly into his hips, and the silken skin of her inner thighs coiled around him like a down quilt. When they rolled over on their sides, her small body curled into a ball in his arms, but her skin was so sleek that it almost seemed she would slip away from him at any moment. Unable to hold her with his arms alone, he bent double like a shrimp and supported her with his whole body, reveling in the indescribable sensation that she was melting around his back and hips like sweet jelly. In the end, even when she was pinned fast beneath him, her small body continued to writhe about, so that every moment brought a new sensation, as if he were sleeping with many different women, each one with a new seduction.

After her flesh itself, the third quality was her attitude. Unlike most geisha—indeed unlike any Japanese woman he'd ever met—she showed neither apprehension nor shame to be seen in the light, be it daylight or lamplight. Any man who so much as made an overture would find her responding even before the futon had been laid out, would see her behave exactly as she might in the dead of night when respectable people are fast asleep. For Kikuchiyo, nightclothes—or even clothing itself—had only one function, to keep out the cold, and they certainly were not meant to hide one's body. There was no denying that Yoshioka had done as he'd pleased in the past, but since he was not a doctor, there was still a great deal he didn't know about the female body, a great many questions he had wanted to ask but never could. Yet now, in one night, thanks to Kikuchiyo, he had all his questions answered, all his frustrations relieved.

Finally, the fourth quality—and one that set her apart from most other geisha—was a flair less as a conversationalist than a teller of improper bedtime stories and erotic anecdotes. Kikuchiyo never talked about her artistic accomplishments or her opinions of famous actors. She never gossiped about other geisha or her employers, and she never spoke ill of the mistresses of the teahouses where she was engaged. Her one and only topic of conversation was herself, but even then the stories were often muddled and disjointed. They were merely accounts of the ways that men had used her, how any number of them had toyed with her from the time she'd first become a maid in a nobleman's house, to her more recent experiences as a geisha. When other geisha did figure in one of these stories, it always concerned their amorous relations with their clients or gossip about what happened in the privacy of the bedroom. It didn't matter whether

Kikuchiyo was talking about travel or a hot spring resort, the theater, the moving pictures, or Hibiya Park, for her there was only one topic of conversation: lovemaking.

If, for example, she happened to mention the Kabukiza, it was to tell a story about a customer who had been up to something rather naughty in a front box while Omodakaya was playing "Kanjinchō," disrupting an entire act. (According to her, this sort of thing has always taken place, and theater people actually approve of it because they think it brings good luck.) Similarly, if the subject of the resort at Hakone came up, she had a tale of a curious mishap she'd experienced there:

"I'd had a bit too much to drink, so I went for a dip in the bath to sober up. I was drowsy and the warm water was delicious. I'd been soaking in the tub for a time when I suddenly bumped up against a very hairy man. I assumed it was my client, since I knew he was as hairy as a bear, and there in the steam and the dark, my body just reacted. Without even opening my eyes, I reached for his hand to pull him to me. I thought I'd give him a special treat, something more than the usual fare—a token of my affection that he'd remember when it came time to calculate my tip; and it seemed like the perfect opportunity, since we were neck deep in hot water and he was clean as a whistle. I suddenly remembered something I'd learned from a client who'd come back from abroad. Why not? They say no good deed goes unrewarded, and there was my tip to consider. You see where this is leading? What an idiot I was! I suppose I got a bit carried away when I realized I was doing something I would never do under normal circumstances, and he didn't seem to mind either. He never once let on that I had the wrong man, and he let me go right ahead and do something no geisha or even a tart would normally do. And in the end, he didn't even warn me—just some violent twitching and an ugly grunt, and there it was. I was just opening my eyes, wondering what to do with the contents of my mouth, when a woman's voice began screeching right in my ear. The three of us looked at each other, and that's when I first realized he was a total stranger and not my client. Ugh! The woman who'd just joined us in the bath was his wife, and it turned out they were newlyweds. I heard later that they divorced soon after that. Nothing quite so awful had ever happened to me before—worse than being taken by a bunch of hoodlums from the front and back at once!" Essentially, all of Kikuchiyo's stories were like this one.

In the course of one night with her, Yoshioka decided that he could never let this woman go, knowing how hard to replace she would be. He even convinced himself that his career thus far in the pleasure quarters, in which he'd taken considerable pride, had merely been an apprenticeship for the moment when he had obtained her favors. There, on the spot, he decided that he would pay off her debt . . . and then take his time thinking about other ways in which to have his revenge on Komayo.

The season had come for putting on the padded *kosode* kimono. Fragrant autumn mushrooms like the *hatsutake* and the *shimeji* were losing their appeal on the tables of the Kagetsu, and at the Matsumoto they already were using once precious *matsutake* in the soup broth. The chrysanthemums that had brought the crowds to Hibiya Park for a time disappeared without a trace, and dead leaves danced in clouds of dust, swirling around the boys playing ball on the empty gravel paths. The new session of parliament opened, and at the teahouses of Shimbashi, along with the usual clients, the uncouth features of provincial visitors and other such outsiders began to appear. The houses were busy night after night due to the stockholders' meetings in Marunouchi and parties for important men of affairs. Talk turned naturally to the subject of the apprentices who hitherto had seemed so young and unripe but who now suddenly made their appearance as full-fledged geisha. The leaves of the willows along the Ginza had turned golden but still clung to the branches. The decorations in the shops had been changed, and the streets were filled with red and blue flags marking the year-end sales. Passersby turned instinctively and then quickened their pace at the noisy strains of street-corner bands. The calls of the paperboys, advertising a special edition, brought to mind the start of the sumo tournament and the trials and tribulations of the wrestlers that in the coming days would fill the pages of the papers. The geisha were beginning to calculate what they would need for their New Year's wardrobes, and even in front of clients they did not hesitate to take their notebooks from their obi and, licking well-used pencils they never bothered to sharpen, write down their engagement schedule for the holiday.

It was only now that Komayo began to realize that Yoshioka had not put in an appearance after that night at the Hamazaki, and she suddenly began to worry that something was wrong. This also was the season for the annual party given by the insurance company where he was employed, and most of the geisha who usually attended were called. Komayo was crushed when she learned the next day that she alone had been omitted, but there was little she could do.

A week after the Shimbashi dance recital, Segawa left with his troupe for a tour of the provinces that would take them from Mito to Sendai and, in all likelihood, keep them away until the end of the year. As always, the star of the revue was Ichiyama Jūzō, who was known for his gruff voice and his grim acting style in the manner of Danzō. And then there was Kasaya Tsuyujūrō, who had once worked in the variety halls and proved invaluable to the company for his ability to play any role, male or female, old or young. Komayo had been sad when Segawa departed, but at least she finally had time to take careful stock of the Yoshioka matter and other things relating to her professional life that she had been ignoring for too long.

There was the master of the Chōmondō, the sea monster of an antique dealer from Yokohama for whom Hanasuke had forcibly procured her at the Taigetsu. He was still showing up every week or so without fail. In the beginning, she had submitted to him in order to save face with Hanasuke; but afterward, finding herself unable to escape, she'd seen him a second and then a third time, and been forced to put up with things that no geisha should have to tolerate—except perhaps Kikuchiyo. She had even tried being cruel to him, thinking that he would lose interest in her despite his easygoing disposition; but nothing seemed to disturb the sea monster and his benign smile. Each time he called her, he would gather a number of popular geisha to serve with Komayo; and apparently with the idea of making a name for her throughout Shimbashi—though much to her distaste—he had called all the senior geisha together during the autumn dance recital and asked them to do what they could for his favorite. In short, his conduct was beyond reproach. He had known all about her affair with Segawa even before she'd told him, but far from objecting, he had sent the actor a ceremonial curtain as a gift. Still—although from a financial standpoint, this one patron was worth a thousand others—the pain and vexation he inspired were a hundred thousand times worse than with an ordinary client. Her body would tremble with disgust, and she always told herself that this time was the last. But once the crisis had passed, her business instincts returned and her resolve weakened, especially toward the end of the month or when she found herself a bit short. It was all a game with him: if she moved back a square, he would attack, cutting off her retreat and pressing his advantage. And when he did, she was in no position to cry out in dismay. No matter what he did to her, she could only turn her head and whimper to herself.

But this distress, the image of a woman clenching her teeth in frustration—this was exactly what the antique dealer from Yokohama found gratifying. He was well aware that his skin was dark and unattractive, and from his youth his success in love had always been based on his overbearing nature. Since there were both *machiai* and geisha houses in Yokohama that were indebted to him, he did not lack for women. Still, he had long been accustomed to a life of amusement, so when he came up to Tokyo he could not rest until he had stopped in at one teahouse or another. The sea monster knew perfectly well that his appearance was no cause for rejoicing among the women of the chosen house, and so in time he came to enjoy embarrassing and tormenting them more than anything else. He became the sort of trying customer who liked nothing better than to force himself on an unwilling woman, and he was constantly pestering the teahouse owners to introduce him to a geisha who was in need of money for her actor or who had got into debt for some other reason. He found it utterly fascinating and amusing to watch them from his position of power as they cried their bitter tears yet nonetheless submitted to his disgraceful demands—all for the love of money. This was the vulgar sport of a man who had risen from vulgar origins.

In this sense, Komayo was ideal for him. No matter how much she might wish to be rid of him, as long as she continued her affair with Segawa there was no way she could shake him off. Thus in December, when people begin to look frantically for any source of money, even the stray coin dropped in the street, to pay their year-end debts, the sea monster, seeing his chance, lumbered off to the Taigetsu and had them call Komayo.

Even though the winter days were short, there still was light in the sky as she made her way down Itajinmichi toward a notions shop she patronized. Passing a house with an electric sign that read "Kikuobana," it suddenly occurred to her that she hadn't visited Kikuchiyo since she'd left to start her own business. Komayo stepped into the entranceway and announced herself. A voice called out from the back, urging her to come in, but Komayo explained that she had some shopping to do and would stop in on her way back. As she was walking away, she passed a covered *rikisha* coming from the other direction. Through the hood she caught just a glimpse of the passenger, but thinking he looked remarkably like Yoshioka-san, she turned to watch as they pulled up in front of the Kikuobana. There was something familiar about the color of the trousers that emerged from under the hood.

"How odd," she thought, "but it couldn't be. . . ." Still, thinking it best to see for herself, she turned cautiously and was heading back when the lattice door of the house clattered open. A girl of fourteen or fifteen emerged, most likely a maid out on an errand. Seeing her chance, Komayo stopped her.

"Was that a guest arriving just now?"

"Yes."

"Your mistress's patron?"

"Yes."

"Well then, I'd better come back some other time. Please give her my regards."

"I will," said the girl, before running off to the saké shop down the street. "A large bottle," she called. "Your best, as usual!" Even though she was on the verge of fainting, Komayo heard the shrill voice quite distinctly.

When she arrived home, she was still too shocked for tears. She'd known nothing until today—the very day she'd unwittingly chosen to pay a call on Kikuchiyo. And now, to think of them sitting there laughing at her expense. . . . It was all too much to bear.

At that moment, O-Sada, the attendant, appeared to inform her that she had an engagement at the Taigetsu. Realizing that the sea monster was waiting for her, her rage grew even greater. She had O-Sada call back to say she wasn't well and would pay the fine for taking the evening off. Then she went upstairs. But after half an hour, apparently having changed her mind, she called for the attendant and left for the teahouse.

A short time later, at about the hour when the lamps were lit, Komayo called her house and asked for Hanasuke.

"I'm going to Mito," she announced. "Please make some excuse to O-Sada and to Jūkichi-san."

"Koma!" Hanasuke blurted out, thinking she was about to hang up. "But where are you now? At the Taigetsu?"

"No, I dropped in at the Taigetsu, but now I'm at the Gishun. I've explained everything to the mistress here. But it's too complicated to call and tell the people there. I'll be back tomorrow or the day after. Something has come up and I need to talk to Segawa-san. So please, I'm counting on you to help."

She was not sure why, but Komayo had suddenly felt a reckless urge to see Segawa's face. Resentment and mortification were raging inside her, and there was no one else to whom she could turn, no one to comfort her. With no thought for the consequences, she had decided to run off to Mito, where Segawa was touring with his company.

12. *Rain on an Autumn Night*

Kurayama Nansō lived a quiet life in his retreat in Negishi, taking pleasure in the passing seasons and the waters surrounding his villa. Here, wagtails and bush warblers appeared in time to take the place of the striped mosquitoes that hid in the shade of the thick undergrowth. The water of a pond had been channeled to form a small stream that flowed past the windows of his study, and on summer nights, when the rush flowers were in bloom, he would gaze out at the fireflies striking like raindrops against the bamboo blinds. In autumn, he would rest his chin in his hands and listen to the rustling of the reeds. Having long since passed into middle age, he now preferred to spend his time contemplating the flowers and trees in his garden, although they often reminded him that the days and months passed with astonishing speed.

In late summer, if he noticed the way the pearly raindrops of evening showers pelted the leaves of the lotus, it seemed only a moment later that he was hearing dry reeds sighing in the wind and autumn had come, with the amaranths giving way to chrysanthemums. Then when the last maple leaves had fallen with the late autumn showers, the year suddenly was over and it was time to count the buds on the plum that bloomed with the winter solstice. During the coldest days, he would take out the night soil and, carefully holding his nose, spread it at the roots of the old trees. It was in that season one knew the plea-sures of winter confinement: a cup of tea brewed in the dead of night or the berries of the nandina and the *yabukoji*, lovelier than flowers against the snow. But then suddenly there were narcissus and adonis on the bookshelf, and before they had faded, the spring equinox had come. Time to thin the chrysan-themums and sow grass seeds. The days are never long enough for one who loves his garden, and Nansō was constantly busy welcoming and bidding farewell to a hundred different kinds of flowers. No sooner did his eyes stop to linger on the fresh green in the treetops than he found the garden darkened by the rainy season, and if the plums ripened and began to fall in the morning, by evening the leaves of the mimosa were rolled up in sleep. Under the bright noonday sun, the pomegranate tree seemed ablaze with blossoms, and the ground was strewn with the petals of trumpet flowers. Late at night, from the shadows of dew-drenched water plants, the threadlike voices of insects warned of autumn's approach.

Spring, summer, fall, and winter—it was truly no different from reading the seasonal poems in a book of haiku. At some point again this year, the same bush warblers that had come last spring started chirping from deep inside the thicket, and the wagtails began their familiar dance at the edge of the pond. In a world where sentiment and fashion were constantly chang-ing, it comforted Nansō to see that these tiny birds returned to his garden each year without fail. He therefore took great care not to disturb them as he pruned away dead branches, forcing his way deeper and deeper into the bushes until he came to the boundary between his own garden and the property next door. It was marked by a tall bamboo hedge dotted with snake gourds. Through a gap, Nansō could see his neighbor's sunlit garden and beyond to the veranda of the main house which looked out over a small pond.

After that, whenever he was walking near the hedge and stopped to glance through the hole, he was invariably captivated by the appearance of the house, the gate of woven bamboo, the shape of the pine branches that hung over the pond—all exactly like a picture in one of the old romances. He often stood gazing in reverie until the striped mosquitoes biting his cheeks brought him back to himself. The house had once belonged to a brothel in the Yoshiwara licensed quarter, but it had stood empty for a long time now. Nansō's own house had been in his family for three generations, and since he had lived here since childhood, he naturally had learned a good deal about the house next door from hearing the old people talk about it. One story had struck him in particular, although the incident itself had taken place while he was still small enough to be held in his mother's arms. The house had been used for rest and recuperation since before the Meiji Restoration, and at the time in question a courtesan had come from the Yoshiwara to recover from an illness. One night, however, in the midst of a heavy snowfall, she died, and Nansō, though still a small child, remembered being strangely moved at this sad ending. Even now, when he saw the way the branch of the ancient pine reached from the bank of the pond to the edge of the veranda, he felt that no matter how old he became, he would never be able to dismiss the old ballads like "Urazato" and "Michitose" as just empty imaginings. No matter how Westernized customs and manners might have become, as long as one could hear the bells on a brief summer night or see the stream of the Milky Way on an evening in autumn, as long as the trees and plants specific to each region remained, then, he was sure, sorrow would remain at the heart of relations between men and women, just as the old ballads said.

By temperament and background, Nansō was destined to be a writer. His great-grandfather, though a doctor by profession, had been a student of the Japanese classics, and his grandfather, also a doctor, had made a name for himself as a satirical poet. By the time his father, Shūan, inherited his patrimony, the family had accumulated considerable property, and had the world gone on as before, a third generation of doctors would have ensured even greater prosperity. But the Restoration overtook Shūan, and traditional Chinese medicine fell completely out of favor. Soon, without really giving it much thought, he had given up his practice and begun to earn his living by engraving inscriptions on seals and monuments, a skill he had originally taught himself as a hobby. It was at about this time that he changed his professional name to Shūsai. A talented poet and fine calligrapher, Shūsai gradually came to be known in all sorts of circles, and for a time he had a certain reputation in the literary world of the capital. So as luck would have it, his income eventually surpassed what he had earned as a doctor, and without even exerting himself, he was able to amass a considerable fortune, large enough, in fact, to ensure that his heirs would not know hardship for many years to come. He died a happy man.

Nansō was twenty-five at the time and already had published a novel or two in the style of Bakin, as serials in the newspapers. Among Shūsai's acquaintances were quite a few publishers and editors, and so it was natural that Nansō became a full-time writer after his father's death. Still, he had no particular affinity for the writers of the Friends of the Inkstone group, like Kōyō or Bizan; he was unacquainted with practitioners of the "new literature," such as Tōkoku, Shukotsu, or Kōchō; and he'd had no occasion to meet men like Shōyo or Futō of the old Waseda circle. Instead he worked alone, taking his inspiration solely from the library kept in the storehouse of his home in Negishi, volumes of Chinese and Japanese classics and collections of essays and jottings from the Edo period. Chikamatsu would serve as his model one day, Saikaku the next, or Kyōden or Sanba. From them he learned the spirit of humility as a writer of "frivolous tales," and for twenty years he had calmly and carefully continued to write his stories, never growing weary of his craft.

Times were changing, though, especially in the first decades of the twentieth century. There were new developments in literature and art, in the theater and in popular music, and even in the rhythms of everyday life. But far from wanting to participate in them, Nansō found more and more occasion for indignation. Nonetheless, for the first time he also seemed to realize that he would not be satisfied to end his days having written nothing but some tales for women and children, and so just as Kyōden and Tanehiko had done in their later years, he immersed himself in the study of the manners and customs and accoutrements of bygone times. In regard to his activities as a novelist, he produced only what was necessary to meet his obligations to the newspapers and publishers with whom he had old ties.

So it was that in Nansō's eyes, the old house and garden in Negishi had come to seem like an irreplaceable treasure. The neighborhood had gradually been developed, and the flavor of old Negishi was about to disappear forever. Although insects had already begun to eat away at the veranda of his ancient house, Nansō knew it was here that his great-grandfather had sat long ago, gazing at the plum blossoms by the pond while reciting from the classics. In later years, it was here that his grandfather had composed his satirical verses as he watched the autumn moon shining down on the sagging tiled roof. The thought made Nansō all the more determined to preserve the old house and garden, no matter how expensive the project might prove to be or how incommodious the place was to live in. The carpenter who came to fix the occasional leak or make other repairs invariably reminded him that in the long run, it would be better to rebuild the house. But Nansō merely laughed; and three years ago when the underpinnings of the foundations had been replaced, he had carefully supervised the work himself, as if he were a carpenter. By the same token, he looked on every tree and plant in the garden as mementos that had once inspired his ancestors to poetry, and he cherished them as no less valuable than the books, utensils, and other objects that were kept in the family storehouse. Fearing that the gardener would do the clipping without due circumspection, Nansō went out each spring and autumn to do the job himself.

This affection was not limited to his own house but extended beyond the fence to the garden next door. The house had stood empty for a long time after the Yoshiwara brothel went bankrupt, and no buyer had been found. Rumors spread that the courtesan who died there had returned as a snow spirit to haunt the house or that foxes and badgers were up to their old tricks, and the prospects for selling the place grew dim. Yet no one in the Kurayama household next door, not even the women and children, had ever regarded the place as strange. On nights when the moon was especially beautiful, having exhausted the charms of a walk in his own garden, Nansō's father, the old Shūsai, had thought nothing of pushing through the gap in the fence to stroll around the pond in the empty garden, loudly reciting ancient Chinese odes to the moon as he went. At other times, when someone came to press him for a piece of engraving work he had failed to finish on schedule, he would slip out of the house and hide in the garden next door, where in due course he would be joined by the maid and his wife, who had searched the house for him and were at a loss for what to tell the customer.

Ultimately, his father had been unable to stand by and watch the branches of the old pine tree by the pond go to ruin from long neglect. Although he knew that the only one to benefit would be some future owner of the property, he began to send his own gardener across the hedge to shake the old needles from the tree or do whatever else might be necessary. On another occasion, the thatched gate was damaged in a storm. Convinced that the craftsmen of the day would be unable to make something similar, no matter how much one was willing to spend, and unable simply to watch it deteriorate, Shūsai had secretly gone to repair it himself. Then one day, he found himself opening the storm shutters and making his way into the house. Was it here that the courtesan had taken her cures or written her letters or burned incense? Perhaps it was just his imagination, but he found the house utterly enchanting, despite its desolate appearance, and fairly often he would have saké brought from his own house so he could drink it there alone. Consequently, the unsold villa came to seem like a second residence to him. Despite persistent rumors that it was haunted, guests at the Kurayama house were taken to the old villa so often that they grew accustomed to it, to the point that one of them was even eager to buy it. This was the kabuki actor Segawa Kikujo, adoptive father of the current Segawa Isshi. As attested to by his friendship with the noted seal-carver, Kurayama Shūsai, Kikujo had a pronounced affinity for the literary life—something quite uncommon in an actor—and taking up residence in rooms that had once belonged to a Yoshiwara brothel, he lived out his days consoling himself from the cares of his profession with the tranquil pleasures of writing poetry and practicing the tea ceremony. After Kikujo's death, his second wife had stayed on in the house until the ceremonies to mark the first anniversary of his death had been performed. But then, being much younger, she elected to move to more convenient quarters in the Tsukiji district, and the house once again fell vacant. It remained in the Segawa family, however, and a gardener was hired to look after it and keep it ready for the occasional visit in spring or autumn.

Nansō's father, Shūsai, had passed away several years before Kikujo, but the connection between the two properties had grown still closer in the succeeding generation. Nansō had established himself as a drama critic at an early age and his name was now quite well known. So soon after Kikujo died, his adopted son, Isshi, began coming almost daily to visit the Kurayama house. Nansō, for his part, welcomed him cordially, since at that time he was nursing a secret ambition to write plays himself.

After Isshi's foster mother moved to Tsukiji, however, the friendship gradually cooled. For Isshi, the trip was a long one and he rarely came to stay at his late father's house, and Nansō's interest in literature and the theater had slowly faded. In a solitary moment, morning or evening, if he took a quiet look at the old garden next door, it was out of a desire to indulge his thoughts of bygone days. He no longer felt a need to see the young actor.

Meanwhile, the garden grew more and more hushed and deserted, blanketed under a deepening carpet of dead leaves. Even in summer and autumn, when the time for trimming came, the sound of shears was never heard. It was silent again, except for the cries of the shrikes in autumn and the bulbuls in winter, just as it had been long ago when Nansō, as a boy, had followed uneasily after his father on their walks here. While he worked away in his own garden, Nansō would often peer through the hedge, and he could only conclude that no one in the Segawa family, neither Kikujo's widow nor Isshi himself, had any interest in the old villa; they were letting it go to ruin as they waited for a buyer to come along.

Nansō no longer harbored any theatrical ambitions nowadays, but his relations with various newspapers made it necessary for him to write theater reviews from time to time. He told himself that should he happen to attend a play in which Isshi was appearing, he might like to go backstage and renew their long-interrupted acquaintance and thus perhaps bring up the subject of the house next door. If the occasion seemed right, he might even go a step further and suggest that if the house had to be sold, it would be better to sell it to someone who could appreciate its worth. It was his sense of family connection that made him want to give this advice. After all, hadn't his own father, unbeknownst to anyone, taken care of the old pine tree and the thatched gate? But then, thinking it over, he doubted whether this sort of information would have any effect. Nowadays, even the grandest old families, such as the Date of Sendai, didn't hesitate to sell off hereditary treasures that had been accumulated over many generations, even when there seemed no pressing need to do so. Indeed, it now was quite fashionable to convert such possessions into hard currency, so Nansō thought it best to keep silent on the matter. Nonetheless, as the days and months passed, when he made his morning and evening inspections across the fence, he wondered apprehensively when a new owner would appear or when the pine by the pond would be dug up and carried off.

One night, the rain outside his window pattered on the dry lotus leaves. Gathering up the books that lay scattered about and straightening the papers on his desk, Nansō decided it was nearly time for bed. He had filled his silver pipe one last time and was listening to the rain as he smoked when suddenly he thought he heard the strains of a shamisen. He listened more carefully.

It wasn't that one never heard a shamisen in the neighborhood, but the piece being played struck him as odd. It seemed to be a ballad from the Sonohachi repertoire, sung by a woman with a captivating voice. Nansō, who had a taste for such things, opened the round window to get a better view, only to be still more surprised. There appeared to be a light in the house next door. which he had assumed was still vacant, and the Sonohachi piece, the particularly pathetic "Ballad of Toribeyama," sounded even more melancholy, coming to him through the drizzling rain from across the garden.

The whole effect was so strange that Nansō felt after all these years, perhaps now the house really was haunted by a restless spirit. If the singer had been performing a Kiyomoto ballad or something from the *nagauta* repertoire, he wouldn't have felt so disquieted, despite the rainy, cheerless night. But this was Sonohachi, the most somber of the *jōruri* styles, reserved for dreamlike stories of love suicides told in the most plaintive tones. Reluctantly, he decided it must be the spirit of the courtesan who had died in the house. Unable to rest in peace, she had returned on a rainy night to sing to herself her secret lament at being still bound to this world.

Quietly, the door to the study slid open. "I've made you some tea, dear," his wife said. Nansō turned abruptly.

"O-Chiyo, something funny is going on."

"What do you mean?"

"It seems there *is* a ghost over there after all."

"Don't say that!"

"But listen. There! Can't you hear someone singing a Sonohachi ballad in the empty house next door?"

A look of relief came over her face. "You can't scare me like that. I already know more about it than you do."

Nansō was puzzled to find his easily frightened wife behaving with such calm. "You know about the ghost?"

"Of course. Haven't you seen her yet?"

"No."

"Well, she's about twenty-four or twenty-five. She seems younger, but I suspect she's older than she looks. Her cheeks are round and her skin is a bit dark. I'm sure you'd find her delightful. She's a charming girl in full flower." O-Chiyo paused and listened for a moment. "And she has a lovely voice. Do you suppose she's also playing the shamisen?"

His wife had no direct ties to the world of musicians and entertainers, but when it came to styles of music such as Sonoha-chi, Katō, Itchū, or Ogie, she knew a great deal more than the average geisha. This was because she had been born into the family of a celebrated dilettante painter who had lived for a time in great luxury, and she had grown up in the company of the painters, writers, actors, and entertainers who came to visit her father. It was almost twenty years ago that she'd come to Kurayama's house as a young bride, and she now was a woman of thirty-five with two children. Yet even today, when she did her hair up in the ginkgo-leaf style and went out shopping, she still was occasionally mistaken for a geisha. Her youthful temperament, carefree attitude, and generous spirit were utterly unlike Nansō's subdued character, but somehow this contrast became the basis of their harmonious life together.

"O-Chiyo, how did you come to know all this? Have you been spying?"

"No, I came by my information quite honestly. But I'm not going to reveal my sources so easily." She laughed but, coming closer, soon began to tell her story. This evening, as she was arriving home from her shopping, two covered *rikisha* had pulled up behind her and lowered their poles at the gate of the house next door. Thinking it rather unusual, she had turned around just in time to see Segawa Isshi emerge from one and, from the other, a lovely young woman who appeared to be a geisha. "It's perfect, don't you think?" she concluded, beginning to laugh again. "What better way to escape prying eyes?"

"It is quite clever. They probably found it necessary because Segawa is so popular these days." Nansō was laughing too.

"I wonder whether she's a geisha or perhaps someone's mistress?"

"The rain seems to have just about stopped. Would you light a lantern for me? I'm going to have a look."

"I don't think you have to go to that much trouble," she said. But the next moment she had gone to the cupboard on the veranda. She found a lantern and lit it.

"Are the children asleep?"

"I'm sure they are. They went to bed a long time ago."

"Then why don't you come with me? The lantern bearer gets to walk in front, you know."

"Well, the rain has stopped at just the right time for it." She had already slipped into her garden clogs and was standing on the stepping-stone by the veranda, holding up the light for him. "It's like something out of a play," she giggled, "and I'm the loyal chambermaid."

"Out in the garden by lamplight—it is rather fun, isn't it? I suppose I might play the prince from the 'Tale of the Twelfth Chapter.' No, the scene we're doing tonight is a more sordid tale of jealousy, about a man who leads his wife out to spy on the house next door." Nansō broke into laughter as he finished.

"Not so loud! They'll hear you!"

"Can you hear the crickets? It seems sad that so many are still alive and singing. O-Chiyo, you can't get through that way. There's always a puddle by the pomegranate. It's better to slip under the myrtle."

Following the stepping-stones, they made their way into the underbrush. O-Chiyo shielded the lantern with her sleeve and held her breath, but the Sonohachi music died away, leaving only the faint light shining through the paper doors of the veranda. They could hear nothing, no voices, no laughter, only the desolate silence.

But the next morning, the sky was clear and brilliant after the rain. In the warmth of the Indian summer, steam rose in clouds from the damp earth and the moss-covered roofs. Nansō was out planting bulbs of Chinese narcissus under the plum tree and around the garden rocks when suddenly he realized that now he was the one being spied on, as Segawa Isshi called to him through the fence. "Sensei! As diligent as ever, I see."

Reaching up with a muddy hand to pull his old hat from his head, Nansō made his way toward the voice.

"I don't understand why we haven't met up till now. How long have you been here? I had no idea you'd come."

"I arrived only yesterday, for a short rest. I'm sorry I didn't come to see you sooner."

"It's been quite a while. Why don't you come over for a talk? My wife often mentions you. We won't make a fuss—why don't you both come?" Nansō lowered his voice. "To be honest, I was rather moved last night. She has a lovely voice."

"You heard her? Then I suppose I should explain."

"I would very much like to meet her," Nansō said, but at that moment a voice called from the veranda.

"Nii-san, where are you?"

"Sensei, let's have a proper talk later. There are a few things I'd like to ask your opinion about." With that Segawa moved away from the fence and headed back toward the house. "I'm over here," he called. "What is it?"

13. The Road Home

It was not until two days later that Segawa dropped in to see Nansō, apparently after the departure of the woman they'd heard singing. The actor answered Nansō's questions quite frankly, and they talked of various things.

"The woman? She's from Shimbashi. You must know her. Her name is Komayo."

"Komayo of the Obanaya? I thought I'd heard that voice before. I've seen her dance many times, but I didn't know she sang Sonohachi. She's very good."

"She's been practicing a few passages lately."

"So, my friend, this time it seems to be serious. I've been hearing the occasional rumor since the end of last year. Can we assume that you're about to take a wife?"

"Actually, I've been thinking it's time, but as long as my mother's alive, it won't be easy."

"I see what you mean. But you should realize that a woman who won't listen to her mother-in-law won't listen to her husband, either. When it comes to marriage, you have to put aside your feelings and think carefully about the whole matter."

"I agree with you. But my mother is still young—just fifty-one this year—and I have a feeling it's going to be difficult to work things out. In fact, I've already taken Komayo to see her a few times. Mother says she seems willing and pleasant enough, but she thinks an actor's wife needs to be more lively and resourceful, especially where matters of property are concerned. 'It might work while I'm still alive,' she says, 'but once I'm gone you could have no end of trouble.' And I suppose she could be right, but I think what really bothers her is that Komayo is a Shimbashi geisha and still has her debt to pay. I'm sure I've told you about my mother. She's part of that frightening class of Kyoto women who are tighter than bill collectors. When it comes to money, there's no reasoning with her."

"I suppose not."

"It's really my father's fault. When his first wife died, why did he have to go all the way to Kyoto to find a second? Aren't there enough women in Tokyo? I mean, where was his loyalty to the spirit of Edo?"

"Perhaps so, but you were lucky she wasn't a rank amateur

with no taste or experience. It's a shame what can happen to an acting clan when it's left in the hands of women from 'good families.' Look at the Narita. It's tragic to see a fine old name like theirs ruined."

"Still, you can't trust Kyoto women, even the professionals. For that matter, why are all women so calculating? Once you're in their debt, even a little bit, they never let you forget it."

"Well, you know what they say: women and bookkeepers are nothing but trouble."

"True enough. But honestly, the only reason I'm thinking about marrying Komayo is that she's always reminding me how much she's lost because of me."

"Then you're not in love? That does change things."

"I don't mean I don't like her. And I didn't go on calling for her just out of a sense of duty. But I have to admit that I'm not absolutely dying to marry her."

Nansō laughed. "That doesn't sound too encouraging, does it?"

"But that's the way I honestly feel. I don't intend to remain single forever, and if the right opportunity were to come along, I'd be happy to take advantage of it. . . . But Komayo—she lost an important patron at the end of last year because of me; and then, out of spite, the man took up with Kikuchiyo from the same house and almost immediately set her up in a place of her own. To get back at him, Komayo insisted that I marry her, even if it was just for a few days. She made a fuss and told me she'd kill herself with morphine if I ever left her. I didn't know what to do, but I finally managed to put her off by telling her it would have to wait until after the memorial services for my father's thirteenth anniversary."

"Ah, the plight of beautiful people. I wouldn't want to be in your shoes."

"Please, don't make fun of me. I just didn't want to be cruel. But I could hardly take her home with Mother there, and taking her to a teahouse where we would be recognized might have hurt her professionally. After thinking through all the possibilities,

I finally realized this villa was empty and we could be together without anyone disturbing us."

"It is nice and quiet here, isn't it. As a matter of fact, I've been meaning to ask you for some time whether you plan to keep it as a second house."

"Well, I suppose so, for the time being, since no one seems interested in buying it. Mother says it would be bad if word got out that we wanted to sell and we fell into the clutches of some real-estate broker."

"You should let it be, then. You can always sell it later if you want to. It's better to leave it just as it is until you find a buyer who loves it and truly wants it. If you go to a broker, he'll set the price for the land as if the house were a worthless ruin. But someone who knows about such things can see the value in every part of the villa, the old doors and windows, the pillar in the *tokonoma*, even the paper on the sliding doors. You really should keep it as it is for the time being. It's bound to become more valuable with age."

"If it isn't too much trouble, I wonder if you'd be willing to look after it? In fact, Mother told me to ask whether you'd consider it, as an old friend, if I happened to run into you at the theater. I'd just forgotten to mention it."

"Really? Of course, and I assure you I'll do my best." With that, forgetting completely about Komayo and Segawa's problems, Nansō launched into an enthusiastic discussion of the beauties of the thatched gate and the pine tree in the garden.

Segawa had intended to take his leave from Nansō before sunset and return to his home in Tsukiji for a good night's sleep in preparation for the beginning of a run at the Shintomi Theater the following day. Consequently, lost as he was in the conversation with his neighbor, he was startled to find the sun setting on the Indian summer day. Then, just as he thought he might get up to go, dinner was served and he stayed on. It was past eight o'clock when he finally emerged from the side door of Nansō's house beneath a luxuriant growth of winter bamboo. A cold wind blew down the darkened street. The moon shone over the woods in Ueno, and there was something infinitely sad about the distant echo of a train and its forlorn whistle. Until he left Nansō's house, Segawa had been thinking it was too far to go home to Tsukiji, given the late hour, and that it might be amusing to spend the night alone in the empty villa. But now he changed his mind and hurried off toward the streetcar stop. As he waited for the streetcar from Minowa, he wondered how anyone could live in such a dark, remote place as this. It might suit a writer like Nansō or a painter perhaps, but he couldn't help thinking that his foster father, Kikujo, must have been quite eccentric to move to such an inconvenient spot in pursuit of the tea ceremony and his other interests. He found himself comparing his own character and artistic technique with his father's and the world he lived in with the one Kikujo had known.

Having been raised in the Segawa family, Isshi still specialized in women's roles for the kabuki. But there had been a moment when the newspapers and journals had been full of criticism of the *onnagata*, arguing that women's roles should be played by women and that the fact they were reserved for men was nothing more than a boorish remnant of the Edo-period prohibition on women in the theater. During this time, Isshi had capriciously decided that he no longer wanted to play women—a decision that frequently put him at odds with his father—and even had thought about giving up acting altogether or perhaps joining a theater troupe that performed in the new style and going abroad. In the end, though, this proved to be nothing more than a passing fancy, a whim inspired by the newspapers, and when the debate died down, Isshi quickly forgot all about it. After all, he had trained from childhood to be an *onnagata*, and it was for that role that he was in demand. Without particularly exerting himself, he had accumulated a great deal of experience on the stage and had come to be known as an actor of considerable accomplishment. Just as he began to see himself in the same light, the brief rage for actresses started to fade, and one began to hear the argument that after all, men were most suited to the women's roles in the Japanese theater. This was enough to convince Isshi, and he promptly began placing greater value on his role as an *onnagata* than it might have deserved. As a result, he grew quite demanding and became something of a nuisance to the producers and directors.

"Well, if it isn't Segawa-san. Where have you come from?" A bespectacled man seated near the door of the streetcar greeted him as he got on, tipping his brown velvet hat as he spoke. About thirty, he had the look of a student in his traditional *hakama* trousers.

"Yamai! You've been to the Yoshiwara, I suppose." Laughing, Segawa sat down in the empty seat next to him.

"I'm flattered you think so," said Yamai, laughing in return. "You open at the Shintomiza tomorrow, if I'm not mistaken."

"And I hope to see you there."

"I wouldn't miss it," Yamai said, pulling out a copy from the bundle of journals he had folded under his Inverness. "I've been meaning to send this to you. . . . . It's the magazine I mentioned." The cover of the volume featured the nude figure of a Western woman and the title *Venus, Number 1*. "By subscription only, one yen a month. Absolutely unavailable in bookstores and full of nudes and stories no ordinary journal could publish."

"It sounds quite wild."

"The first issue isn't terribly interesting, but from now on we'll have lots of nude photographs, since paintings already are old hat."

"Better and better! Sign me up!"

"Are you still in Tsukiji 1-chōme?" Yamai took a notebook from his coat and wrote down Segawa's address. He was one of the so-called new artists who used neither pen name nor sobriquet but was known by his real name, Yamai Kaname. Having no more than a secondary school education, he had no particular academic specialization. But he was clever by nature and since his school days had been contributing both traditional and Western-style poems to young people's magazines. Along the way, he had learned the vocabularies of philosophy and aesthetics, so that now he was able to chatter about life and art as glibly as any competent scholar. After high school, together with a few friends, he had managed to convince the foolish son of a wealthy family to finance a new arts magazine he was editing, and then in quick succession he published a series of poems, plays, and novels, so that in the space of three or four years he had established himself as a well-known man of letters. Beyond this, he also had powerful theatrical ambitions, and so trading on the reputation he had made in the literary world, he gathered together a group of actresses and, taking a role himself, staged a number of performances of foreign plays in translation. But the newspapers soon began reporting that he was involved with one of the women, and he was censured for failing to pay the theater owner as well as the wigmaker, the costume designer, and the prop master, among others. As a result, he found himself shunned by the theater world and was forced to return to his original literary pursuits.

Even though he was past thirty, Yamai lived like a student in his twenties. Having no home or wife or children, he went around sponging off one rooming house after another, seemingly without any care for his future. Nor were landlords the only ones he deceived. He was in the habit of accepting advances from publishers when he had no intention of ever writing the book. Or when he did produce something, as soon as it was published he would take the manuscript to another publisher to sell it all over again. It was known that he had often borrowed pages from manuscripts written by his friends and added them to his own work to pad the length and increase the fee. Needless to say, this was done without their permission. His bills at Western-style restaurants, tobacconists, and tailors were never paid, and from Shimbashi, Akasaka, Yoshi-chō, and Yanagibashi all the way to the Yamanote district, he cheated the *machiai* to the limit of his ability. So much so that now, when one of the geisha or teahouse maids he had deceived caught sight of him at the theater or elsewhere, far from trying to collect the debt, she would turn and run out of fear that she might suffer new losses simply by speaking to him. Although it was unclear who had thought it up, he was known to all by the nickname Izumo Tōshū, which sounded like the name of a playwright but also implied that he was "always cheating."

If the world sometimes seems small, it also is quite wide. If it can seem cruel, it also can be generous. So there still were those among the actors and the geisha who had not yet realized how dangerous and untrustworthy Yamai could be, and still others who, though they had already been cheated once or twice, took the charitable view that such behavior was only to be expected from painters or writers. Then there were those who knew all about his faults but still found it interesting to associate with such a low character. Although secretly on guard to avoid falling victim to him themselves, they nonetheless enjoyed hearing his lewd stories—the sort of thing they could never have come up with on their own. So there were those who were willing to buy him a drink in his role as professional rascal, and one of these was Segawa Isshi. As soon as he laid eyes on Yamai, he had been forced to buy his *Venus* magazine with its nude cover, but still his manner was amused.

"Yamai-san, I haven't seen any interesting films lately. Do you still hold those private screenings you used to organize, the 'special' ones?"

"Yes, we still have them," Yamai said, "but I don't run them any more." Then he glanced at Segawa as if he'd just remembered something. "You must know the son of the Obanaya in Shimbashi. He's handling them now."

"The son of the Obanaya? No, I don't know him. I knew Ishikawa Raishichi, the actor who died some years back. Did he have a brother?"

"It's Raishichi's younger brother. He's their real son, but it seems he was practically disowned by the family some time ago.

He's still young, only twenty-two or so, but he has a real genius when it comes to vice. He even puts me to shame."

With that, Yamai launched into a long account of old Gozan's second son.

14. Asakusa

Yamai had become acquainted with the son of the Obanaya at a disreputable bar in the Senzoku-chō district of Asakusa. Yamai was incapable of going straight home to his lodgings from the theater or a dinner. Even when he'd been out on serious business, if the hour grew late he could never bring himself to head in the direction of his boardinghouse but would instead wander aimlessly through one questionable neighborhood or another. When the *machiai* politcly turned him away owing to his debts and a search of his pockets failed to turn up even enough for the *rikisha* fare to the Yoshiwara or Susaki, he had no qualms about spending a drunken night in the most squalid of brothels. Of course, he often was filled with remorse the next day, but his will was no longer able to govern the desires of a body that had been indulged and abused for many years. Yamai would record the various emotions his weaknesses evoked in traditional poems with modern titles such as "The Sorrows of the Flesh" and "The Bitter Taste of Kisses," and he published them without the least sign of embarrassment in a collection he entitled *True Confessions*. To his great good fortune, this work was given a warm welcome by a literary world constantly hungry for novelty, and the careless critics declared that the true poet of the new age was Yamai Kaname. He was dubbed the "Verlaine of Japan," and sometimes when he was in his cups, he was inclined to believe it himself. In his desire for artistic glory, he made ever greater efforts to immerse himself in his degrading habits. Since he had gone no further than high school and even there his marks had been poor, his grasp of foreign languages was tenuous at best. But in his own mind at least, he gradually came to accept that he honestly was some sort of Western writer. Thus when he had contracted syphilis a few years earlier and lesions had appeared, he remembered having read somewhere that the great French writer Maupassant had gone mad from the disease. Even at his lowest ebb, feeling sullied and afraid, the thought that they both were victims of the same scourge filled him with a fierce artistic energy that produced several dozen new poems—which he published under the title *Iodine*. This, too, was well received, and the royalties allowed him to break with his usual custom and actually pay the hospital bill. Such were the stories that were told whenever Yamai's name was mentioned.

At the edge of a foul drainage ditch in Asakusa Park, behind the Hanayashiki amusement center, was a bar marked by a lantern that read "Tsurubishi." On occasion, when Yamai was unable to pay for a geisha at a *machiai* or lacked the ambition for an outing in the Yoshiwara or Susaki, he came here to spend the night. The mistress of the place, a woman of twenty-four or twenty-five by the name of O-Sai, was surprisingly attractive for someone in such an unsavory occupation. She was tall, with a good complexion and beautiful hair. Her bright eyes and thick, arched eyebrows more than compensated for her flat nose and weak mouth, making her well worth a second look. The first time Yamai had happened by, she had called out to him through the lattice window: "So why don't you come in? Yes you, with the glasses." Through the blinds, she might almost have been mistaken for a geisha, with her hair done up in an inverted gingko-leaf style and dressed in a short, redyed jacket with a fine pattern. Convinced that he'd found something rather special, Yamai had hurried into the bar. He made no effort to haggle over the tariff—one yen for a brief visit, three yen to stay the night—and even went so far as to treat her to a dish of river eels before taking his leave the next morning. He went back to see her three or four

times, and then one morning, on his way home from a night in the
Yoshiwara, he suddenly decided to have a drink in Asakusa Park.
Wandering up to O-Saï's place, he found her at the door, grilling
some dried horse mackerel over a hibachi. She was dressed carelessly in a single night robe with a narrow sash tied loosely at the
waist. Seated across from her at a low table with curved legs was a
pale, handsome young man of perhaps twenty-two or twenty-three,
dressed in a padded kimono of some common silk stuff in a brown,
checked pattern. They were drinking saké, but when O-Saï caught
sight of Yamai, she jumped up to embrace him.

"Where have you been? That was cruel, to leave me like that.
But, I'll forgive you this time. Sit down, then, and have a drink."
Before she had even pulled him down to the table, the young
man seemed to have disappeared.

Even though it certainly was not love that had led Yamai to O-
Saï's door, there was something that made him curious about this
customer of hers. In answer to his question, she told him that he
wasn't a customer at all but her younger brother, and pressing
against him even more lasciviously than usual, she dragged him
off to the second floor, a tiny hideaway tucked under the eaves in
the rear and papered tightly on all sides to keep out the soot and
mouse droppings.

Yamai made a furtive escape from the house some time later,
having scraped together one yen for the woman from the coins left
in his pocket from his night in the Yoshiwara. But once outside in
the air and sunlight, he felt quite different. Just as a man who has
filled his belly instantly forgets that he'd been hungry, so Yamai's
calm demeanor, as he strolled beneath the trees in the park with
his cane tucked under his arm, gave no indication that he had just
used his last yen to purchase the favors of a common whore. After
a while he stopped and smoked a cigarette as he studied the ar-
chitecture of the Kannon Temple that rose before him. He looked
like quite the artist as he stood staring at the facade, nor was this
merely a pose. In some magazine or other he had read a review of
the novel *The Cathedral*, by Blasco Ibañez, who was known as "the

Zola of Spain." The book described the lives of people living in the neighborhoods surrounding the cathedral in Toledo, and it now occurred to Yamai that he could write a similar novel set in the environs of the Asakusa Kannon Temple. He was, in fact, in the habit of mining the descriptions of Western literature published in various journals for ideas that could be readily adapted in his own work—a task for which he had a special facility. Yet he never once read any of these works in their original form. This was due, of course, to the fact that he lacked the education to do so; but in the end this proved quite fortunate, since he could never be accused of plagiarism, nor was there any danger that his imagination would be limited by his sources.

He gazed at the temple, lost in thought, until he had almost finished his cigarette. Then, suddenly, someone called out to him from behind.

"Yamai-sensei!"

Startled, he turned. When he caught sight of the person who had addressed him, he was even more surprised and just a little frightened. It was the pale youth who had been breakfasting with O-Sai at the brazier in the Tsurubishi just a short time ago.

"What do you want?" he said, glancing around in all directions.

"I'm sorry if I startled you," said the young man, bowing repeatedly. "Actually . . . I'm the author of a piece that won a prize last year in a magazine . . . and you were on the jury. I've been hoping for a chance to meet you."

Looking somewhat relieved, Yamai lowered himself onto a nearby bench. He would soon learn from the young man that he was named Takijirō and was the younger son of the Obanaya.

Until the autumn of his fourteenth year, Takijirō had lived with his parents—the storyteller Sounken Gozan and the geisha Jūkichi—and had attended a primary school near their geisha house in Shimbashi. But as time went by, in the fall before he was due to enter middle school, his father concluded that it was not in his best interests to keep the boy too long in such an environment, and his mother was forced to agree. After discussing the matter with a number of their patrons, they decided to rely on the kindness of a certain lawyer, a doctor of jurisprudence, who for many years had asked Jūkichi to accompany him in his singing of Itchū ballads, and they sent their son to live with him as a houseboy and student. The doctor maintained a splendid residence in Surugadai, and it was from there that Takijirō began attending middle school. But it was precisely this arrangement that proved to be his downfall. It was natural enough that Gozan was reluctant to keep a young boy in a geisha house—even though it was his home—just as he was reaching the age for serious study. But in the end, instead of entrusting him to a stranger, it would have been better to keep him under his own strict control, in line with the old samurai values to which he stubbornly clung. Later, Gozan and Jūkichi came to regret their decision, but this was, as the proverb puts it, a matter of arriving after the festival is over.

For the first two years of his stay in the lawyer's house, until he was sixteen, Takijirō studied diligently and showed promise as a scholar. But at the end of that year, the lady of the house developed a heart ailment and moved to their country house in Ōmori with her only daughter, and naturally enough, her husband began to spend most of his nights there as well. Eventually, he came to treat the main residence as little more than an office where he would come in the morning to take care of business. But with the master away, the maids and houseboys—all of whom, like Takijirō, were students—began to take advantage of the situation. What's more, it seems that law students are particularly prone to excess, so when five or six of them would get together, an all-night gambling session would quickly ensue. They also competed to see who would be the first to have his way with the maids and the cook, who occupied rooms at the back of the house. As often as not, the grudging losers in this race would then make a point of barging in on the victors in the middle of the night. Meanwhile, those who had won at cards, flush with their winnings, would parade off to the Yoshiwara, to Susaki, Asakusa, or Gundai, or to the brothels in Hama-chō or Kakigara-chō to find women they could buy cheaply.

At first, Takijirō had been frightened by this sort of behavior and had even burst into tears when they dragged him along. But his reluctance proved short-lived. Easily influenced, it took about a year, by the time he was eighteen, for the boy to become an enthusiastic profligate himself. When evening came, he was incapable of staying at home. He would go out to try his luck at seducing the daughters and servant girls of the iceman, the butcher, the tobacconist, or other shopkeepers in the neighborhood. Later, he would compete with the other houseboys to sleep with the maids at home; and even during the day, he did his best to tempt the schoolgirls who rode the same streetcar. Then one night, as he was about to lure the daughter of the local tobacconist behind the Kanda Myōjin Shrine, he had the bad luck to be caught by the police, who were conducting a roundup of juvenile delinquents. Before he knew what was happening, he'd been arrested. Quite naturally, the incident was reported to his school, and he was immediately expelled. At the same time, he was politely asked to leave the lawyer's house.

His parents were bitterly disappointed and ashamed, but there was nothing to be done. For the time being, Takijirō was taken back into the geisha house in Shimbashi. His father told him he was a disgrace to the family and confined him strictly to home, but he was no longer the Takijirō who had once scrupulously obeyed his parents. In any case, there was no one in the house to enforce the old man's orders. Gozan himself left for his afternoon performance every day after lunch, carrying with him an enormous bag that held his faded, five-crested *haori* jacket and the large fan he would beat on the lectern when the audience's attention wandered. In general, he would return home at dinnertime only to leave again almost immediately for the evening show, but on some days he went directly from the matinee to the later performance. As a geisha, Jūkichi, too, was busy every evening with her engagements. The oldest son of the Obanaya, the actor Ichikawa Raishichi, was still alive at the time, but regardless of whether or not he had a performance, he would leave for his teacher's house right after breakfast and never returned until after ten o'clock at night.

To the casual observer, a geisha house might have appeared chaotic, but anyone who took the trouble to go inside and look around would soon see that everyone—from the master and mistress to the house geisha, the attendant, and on down to the scullery maids—was busy with his or her appointed tasks. Although Jūkichi, the mistress, might have been out at engagements until midnight or even one o'clock the night before, she had to be up early for her own music lessons. Every morning, she attended the practice sessions conducted by the masters of the various schools of singing—Tokiwazu, Kiyomoto, Itchū, Katō, Sonohachi, Ogie, and Utazawa—and when she returned, she had to teach the apprentice geisha in her house. Then there were the regular geisha who needed help with their kimono and any other problems they might have. She also was responsible for making arrangements with geisha from other houses for the songs that were to be played at their engagements. As a senior geisha in the quarter, she was required to help with rehearsals whenever there was to be a public performance. In the midst of all this activity, it soon was time to do up her hair and go to the bath; and before she could even sit down for a quiet smoke, she had to see to dinner. The geisha who lived in the house were nearly as busy, and the attendant, who had to keep the accounts, answer the telephone, and give the geisha a hand with their kimono and accessories, had work enough for two people. Even the maids, what with cooking and washing and drawing baths for so many, had no time to rest.

In fact, with a demanding master like Gozan—a man so quick to find fault that he was known as Kobei the Scold after a famous tale in the storyteller's repertoire—the Obanaya was unsurpassed in Shimbashi for the scrupulousness with which it dealt with every aspect of its affairs. Furthermore, the house had long been famous for the grueling training its geisha received in the arts of their profession—a training that was said to be as rigorous as any school of swordsmanship. This, too, was said to reflect the obstinate and irascible character of Gozan, a man incapable of doing anything in moderation. Even though he was among the most senior of storytellers, he did not have a single apprentice, and it was said that no one came to study with him precisely because the training he provided was too severe. Likewise, he insisted that the geisha who learned their arts in his house practice like true professionals. Quite often the sound of shamisen coming from the upper floors of nearby houses would make him wince. "What in the world is that?" they would hear him say. He said that geisha and actors were the flowers of society, and he warned his charges that it would be to their undying shame if they ever met with some accident outside and were found to be less than impeccable in their attention to their appearance. "When you open the door to step out into the street, be sure that your underclothes are faultless—it isn't those fancy kimono or accessories that matter." Such were the precepts of Gozan's house. But his wife was as tolerant and kind as a person could be and always found a way to soften his eccentric remarks and keep peace not only with the geisha but with the rest of the household as well.

In this house where everyone was kept busy night and day, Takijirō alone had absolutely nothing to do but sit yawning as he read the newspapers and magazines that lay scattered about. Although he was still too young for military service, Gozan thought that the boy might mend his ways if he were severely admonished now and that he might yet discover some aim in life. Since he'd been expelled, there was no point in thinking about more schooling, but hoping to find him a place with a respectable merchant, Gozan had made inquiries here and there. When it was learned, however, that he was the son of a geisha-house owner and that he'd been sent away from school, the efforts came to nothing. "Like father, like son," Jūkichi intoned, suggesting that they train him in one of the performing arts, even though he already was rather old to start on such a course. It was not enough, though, simply to say he should become a performer; they still had to decide what art he would study. Even for Takijirō, this was not something that could be decided on the spur of the moment. His older brother was already a well-known actor, and at this late date, it would be too humiliating to become a player of bit parts, lost in his shadow. Becoming Gozan's pupil would be still worse, since in addition to a father's scoldings, he would have to put up with a master's strenuous discipline. As for the shamisen, he was far too old to start from the beginning now and he did not seem to have any interest in becoming an actor in the new theater or in apprenticing himself to a comedian with the Soga-no-ya troupe. One day, as he was reading one of the journals that happened to come his way, it suddenly occurred to him that it might be interesting to be a novelist or a literary man of some sort. But having no notion at all of how one might embark upon this path, this plan, too, vanished like smoke. So it was that Takijirō, having no idea what to do with himself, decided to go to live and work at a brokerage house that had agreed to hire him, on the off chance that in the process, he might reform himself.

He had been working there satisfactorily for just six months when he embezzled a small sum from the firm to purchase the favors of a prostitute in nearby Kakigara-chō. His crime was quickly detected, and he was fired. Once again, he was taken in at the house in Shimbashi, but he was unable to endure his parents' strict control for more than a few days. One evening when the house was deserted, he gathered up some kimono and hair ornaments that belonged to his mother and the other geisha and fled.

15. At the Gishun

Before Yamai could finish his long story about Takijirō, the tramcar arrived in Ginza. When Segawa stood up abruptly to get off, Yamai followed him. Then when Segawa stopped in front of the Hattori watch shop to wait for the tram to Tsukiji, he found that Yamai was still there beside him.

"Where do you live?" Segawa asked.

"In Shiba Shirokane."

"And you use this stop?"

"No, I usually get the tram at Kanasugibashi in Shiba," Yamai said, coming a step closer. "But what time is it? Still a bit early to be heading home, don't you think?"

"It's not quite ten," Segawa said, checking the gold watch on his wrist with the watches in the shop window.

"How are things in Shimbashi? I haven't been there lately. . . ." Two tramcars went by, but Yamai remained at Segawa's side and seemed to have no intention of getting on.

Segawa finally realized what the man had in mind: he wanted to be taken somewhere and entertained. The prospect of such an evening held no appeal for him, and yet somehow he found it difficult simply to feign ignorance and leave Yamai in the lurch. After all, he thought, giving can benefit the giver, and if he treated him to a drink or two tonight, it might prove to his advantage at some later date. So he asked him whether he felt like "unwinding" somewhere for a while.

Without further delay, Segawa set out across the tracks toward the other side of the street. Beaming, Yamai followed, as if pursuing a bird he feared would get away, and it was amusing to see the care he took to call out warnings about approaching cars. As Segawa walked quickly past the Lion Beer Hall, he glanced back at his companion.

"Do you have a favorite place?" he asked.

"I suppose I do, but the ones I go to are rather shabby—not the sort of spots you'd want to be seen in. Tonight, I'd like to be shown *your* 'port in a storm,' so to speak." Yamai laughed. "And I promise to keep it secret."

Segawa slowed his pace and cocked his head to one side, as if unsure where to go. But they soon arrived at Miharabashi, and reluctantly he seemed to come to a decision.

"The one I go to isn't particularly elegant, either. But for real fun, a cozy hideaway always seems better than one of the deluxe places."

Segawa took Yamai to his usual haunt, the Gishun *machiai*. The maid there, O-Maki, led them to the front room on the second floor. Kneeling, she greeted them with a deep bow and then lowered her voice in a conspiratorial way.

"A call came for you just a moment ago."

"Who was it?"

"As if you didn't know! I'll tell her to come," she said, rising to go to the phone.

"O-Maki," Segawa said. "Call Komayo, then, but get someone else as well."

"And who should that be?" Kneeling again, she looked inquiringly at both of them.

"Yamai-san, who would you like?"

"We can decide that once Komayo comes, but let's have some saké now."

"Very well," the maid said. "I'll bring some immediately." She rose and left the room.

"Geisha are odd creatures," Yamai observed. "If you invite two from feuding houses, it can spoil the whole party." Seeming to have decided to make himself at home, he sat cross-legged with his elbows resting on the rosewood table.

"You can't always tell from appearances, but all women are uncompromising."

"I suppose that's what they call 'feminine nature,'" Yamai said, taking some sweets from a bowl on the table. "By the way, I've been hearing rumors that you're going to be married soon. Is it true?"

"To Komayo?"

"That's what I heard."

"Is that so? I had no idea there was so much gossip. How embarrassing."

"There's nothing to be embarrassed about. You're happy about it, aren't you?"

"Well, I'm no expert, but I don't think marriage sounds very exciting. To be honest, I think I'd prefer to stay single for a while longer yet. Not that I have anything against her in particular," Segawa added, as if convincing himself. "That's a different matter entirely."

Yamai shared a vague sense that marriage was a peculiarly oppressive institution that would spell the end of the splendid freedom he had enjoyed thus far in life.

"There's no reason to rush into it—you can marry any time you like. In the end, though, I suppose it's something everyone should experience at least once."

O-Maki returned with saké and something to eat.

"Komayo-san called to say that she'll be here in half an hour."

"When they say 'half an hour' they mean an hour and a half. In the meantime, O-Maki, we'd like you to call someone who can come right away. Shimbashi geisha always keep you waiting."

"And no sooner do they arrive than they get called away to the next engagement!" Yamai was laughing again. His history of cheating houses all over town had made him something of an expert.

"It's true," O-Maki sighed, sounding sympathetic. Then she seemed to remember something. "There is a girl making her debut tonight. Shall I call her, to pass the time? She's quite shapely and nice looking, quite a lady, in fact." She laughed. "I hear she's actually the wife of an important doctor."

"How odd! Then why would she want to be a geisha?"

"I've heard only rumors, but they say she was fascinated by the idea and absolutely had to see how it felt."

"Is that so? Well, then, we should see how she came out. Yamai-san, do you suppose this is what they call the 'New Woman'?" Segawa's question seemed quite serious.

"No doubt. A good number of the women who bring me their poetry to correct would have no problem becoming geisha."

"I envy you writers," Segawa said. "First, you're not tied to a schedule, and then when you go out to have fun, you can do what you like without attracting attention. Actors are recognized immediately wherever we go, and then we have to behave ourselves. It's a bore, really."

"On the other hand, you don't have to worry about being given the cold shoulder."

"Oh, actors aren't always welcomed with open arms, either." Both of them were laughing now.

Before long, the door to the room slid open quietly to reveal the chignon of a woman bowing at the threshold—no doubt the geisha O-Maki had mentioned. She was dressed in a dark, crested kimono with an elaborate design at the hem, and the white collar of her underkimono was visible at the neck. A young woman of perhaps twenty, there was no fault to be found with her straight hair, thick eyebrows, and large, dark eyes. But her forehead was too broad and her jaw too short, making her face look round. Her large, ample body and plump hands were clearly ill suited to the debutante's kimono; her hair was oddly arranged; and her face too heavily caked with powder—but it was precisely these points of departure from the typical geisha that drew their interest. Still, there was nothing timid about her, and when Yamai offered her a cup of saké, she accepted it without hesitation.

"I hurried, so I'm all out of breath," she apologized. Draining the cup, she handed it back with a "thank you" in English. Her accent was striking—strong and yet somehow unidentifiable.

"What's your name?"

"I'm Ranka."

"Ranka . . . sounds vaguely Chinese, doesn't it? Why didn't you choose something more stylish?"

"Actually, I wanted to call myself Sumire, but that already was taken."

"And have you been working somewhere else? Yoshi-chō? Yanagibashi?"

"No," she said, her voice rising inexplicably, "of course not!" Although her accent grew even stronger, she seemed oblivious to it. "This is my first time as a geisha."

"Then you were an actress, perhaps?"

"No, but I'd like to be. Maybe if I don't succeed as a geisha, I'll try acting."

Segawa exchanged a look with Yamai, then burst out laughing.

"And if you were an actress, what role would you like to play?"

"I'd like to play Juliet," Ranka answered, apparently not in the least intimidated. "In that Shakespeare play—the scene at the window where the birds are singing and she and Romeo kiss— it's wonderful! I don't like Matsui Sumako's *Salome*, though. It's like she's naked on the stage, but I suppose she's wearing a body suit, isn't she?"

Segawa was silent, somewhat overcome by all this, but Yamai, who had been drinking steadily, could hardly conceal his delight.

"Ranka, you'd be wasting your talents as a geisha. By all means, take up acting! If you do, I'll do everything I can to help you. I'm an artist myself, you see, and we artists have to stick together!"

"Really? You're an artist? What's your name?"

"Yamai Kaname."

"What? You're Yamai-sensei? I have every book of poetry you've ever written."

"Is that so?" Yamai said, more and more pleased. "Then you must write poetry yourself. Why don't you recite something for us?"

"Oh no, I don't write, that's beyond me. But when you're sad, reading poetry is such a comfort, don't you think?"

Utterly amazed by now, Segawa puffed away at his pipe, studying the two of them through a cloud of smoke.

16. *Opening Day (I)*

At the appointed hour of one o'clock, the new production at the Shintomiza opened. The program began with the "Badarai" scene from the *Ehon taikoki*, followed by the tenth act from the same play. These pieces had been staples in the repertoire of Ichiyama Jūzō from his days in the juvenile theater when he played the lead role in the style of the old Mikawa star and thereby secured his reputation in the theatrical world as a prodigy. But today the audience was full of expectation at the news that Segawa Isshi, who was known for playing female roles, would, for the first time, be taking the male part of Jūjirō. The third piece, which came abruptly as an interlude unrelated to the play, would be "Crossing Lake Biwa," done with sets in the style of the motion pictures as a sort of theatrical sleight of hand. In the middle of the program came the "Fox Fire" scene from *Nijūshikō*, and the second half would be *Kamiya Jihei*, which featured the Osaka actor Sodezaki Kichimatsu. Since all the seats, from the pit to the boxes, were priced at fifty sen for the opening performance, the house was full, even though everyone knew that the scene changes would be exceptionally long and the usual vignettes would be omitted. "Sold out" signs were soon being posted in the box office and at the teahouses in the quarter where tickets were sold.

By the time the great drum had begun to beat backstage to summon the audience, Komayo already had distributed tips to the three or four attendants she knew at the crowded teahouse. She had called Tsunakichi, Segawa's manservant, and had given him an excessively large gratuity, and she also had handed out the proper considerations to the man who managed the dressing rooms and to the guard who watched the stage door, in order to be able to come and go as she pleased, as if she were an actor's wife. Furthermore, since Segawa would be playing the masculine role of Jūjirō for the first time, she had canvassed her acquaintances throughout Shimbashi to raise money for a commemorative curtain to present to the theater, and thus she had found herself offering tips to the carpenters and stagehands as well.

Komayo had invited Hanasuke to accompany her, and they took their seats in a third-tier box on the right side of the theater. Now, as the "Badarai" scene was ending, she looked out at the full house and thought to herself that it was all due to the popularity of one man, and that man was none other than Segawa Isshi. But even more, the thought that she, Komayo, was the woman who loved and was loved by this famous actor filled her with a numbing happiness. But when she realized that she had no idea when they would be able to live openly as man and wife, she suddenly felt quite miserable.

"Komayo-san, I wanted to thank you for your generosity." The box stood open, and the bustle of latecomers could be heard beyond the figure kneeling quietly in the doorway. It was the wrinkled Kikuhachi; an apprentice under Kikujo, Isshi's father, he had been with the Segawa family for many years. "The master has just arrived," he added.

"Thank you," Komayo said, tucking her tobacco pouch back into her obi. "Hana-chan, they say he's arrived. Let's go and pay him a visit."

True to her subordinate role, Hanasuke said nothing but followed docilely as Komayo left the box. Kikuhachi was escorting them through the crowd toward a curtained door that led to the undercroft beneath the stage when they were stopped by a short, bespectacled man wearing a Western-style suit.

"Komayo-san!"

"Why, Yamai-san! How did things end up last night?"

"Well, she proved to be quite a geisha, that woman."

"Don't think you can get around me so easily," Komayo laughed. "You seemed quite taken with each other." Komayo had met Yamai for the first time that night, but since Segawa had brought him along, she made a show now of giving him a warm reception. Komayo made no distinctions: whenever she met one of Segawa's acquaintances, she did her best to be amiable, to make it plain to everyone how she exerted herself on the actor's behalf. In this way, she hoped, she would gradually attract the sympathy of all those around them, so that later, come what may, these friends would insist on his marrying her. When she learned that Yamai was a writer, Komayo decided that he might be a particularly reliable ally, and it seemed to her only reasonable that she should offer him an evening or two of amusement in return. Being a woman with little knowledge of the world, she believed that such people made a business of writing about the details of human feelings in much the same way that lawyers made a business of the law, and therefore one could safely seek their help in matters of the heart.

"While I was about it, I thought I might tell Segawa about last night," Yamai said, following Komayo into the area under the stage.

They made their way through the dark undercroft, lit here and there by gas lamps, and emerged into the opening-day crush in the dressing rooms. Stagehands ran frantically up and down the stairs, some in black uniforms and others with their kimono tucked up in their sashes. Clutching Hanasuke's hand, Komayo led the way to a room at the left of the stairs. Above the door was a plaque bearing the name Segawa Isshi. As the door slid open, they were greeted by Tsunakichi, Segawa's personal servant, who was boiling water on a brazier in one corner of the tiny antechamber. When he saw Komayo, he instantly rose to set out cushions in the inner room. Her generous tips had had their effect.

Segawa, wearing a padded dressing gown of striped silk and a plain, narrow obi, sat cross-legged on a large crimson cushion at a red lacquer dressing table. He was dissolving the white powder for his makeup when he caught sight of them in the mirror.

"My apologies for last night," he said, greeting Yamai first. Then he turned to Hanasuke. "Do have a seat," he said courteously.

"Yes, do sit down," Komayo echoed, urging her toward one

of the cushions. Komayo, however, made a point of refusing her cushion and kneeling on the tatami slightly to one side. When Tsunakichi brought the tea, she took the tray from him and set a cup before Yamai first, exactly as a good wife would do.

"So what happened after I left?" Segawa said, wiping the powder from his fingertips. "Did you end up spending the night?"

"No, I did get home eventually." Yamai smirked. "But it was around 3:00."

"And we're supposed to believe that?"

"Under the circumstances, she couldn't have let him go home, could she, dear?" Komayo looked at Segawa.

"I can see you think I'm lying," Yamai laughed. "But I have to admit, she's quite an original. You do meet the strangest geisha in Shimbashi from time to time. It seems she never did realize that you're an actor."

"You can't be serious," Komayo said, her eyes widening in surprise.

"I rather prefer it that way," said Segawa. Putting out his cigarette in the ashes of the brazier, he pulled the dressing gown from his shoulders and began applying makeup to his face and neck. Using both hands, he worked with accustomed ease. The company fell silent, their eyes fixed on the mirror, while Komayo, lost in contemplation, seemed to lean forward as if drawn to Segawa's reflection.

"Yamai-san, we should go out again sometime." As Segawa spoke, he quickly sketched on eyebrows and applied rouge to his lips. When he was finished, Tsunakichi had his costume and accessories ready. Segawa rose to slip into a splendid broad-shouldered formal robe with a bellflower crest embroidered in gold. The hairdresser, approaching from behind, added a wig with a forelock and a large topknot, and in an instant the actor was transformed into a handsome youth even more appealing than those in woodblock prints. Komayo longed to be able to play the role of the heroine, Hatsugiku, and to press herself against him, as she might well have done if they had been alone. She managed to resist the urge, but she couldn't keep her eyes off him, bewitched as she was by the sight. This resplendent young man was so different from the female characters she was used to seeing him play. To a woman in love, he would already have held enough attraction, but this was almost more than one could bear. Komayo let out a quiet breath, thinking to herself that the great love she felt for him was almost a kind of suffering. Segawa, however, seemed oblivious to her feelings.

"Tsunakichi," he said, sounding slightly petulant, "isn't it my turn yet?" He rose, his half-smoked cigarette still between his lips.

Just then they heard the voice of the attendant who had been arranging the sandals at the entrance to the dressing room. At the sound of his polite greeting, they turned to find an elegant woman standing in the doorway. Her hair was cut short and she wore a plain, steel blue jacket. "My congratulations!" she said to Segawa as she made her way into the room. Komayo, as if astonished at this entrance, slid off her cushion and bowed deeply, speaking up before anyone else had time to answer.

"How good of you to come! I apologize for not having come to see you."

It was Ohan, Kikujo's second wife and Isshi's stepmother.

Her oval face was complemented by large eyes and a fine, straight nose. Her hair had been cut in a style suitable for a widow, but her complexion was pale and smooth, with no noticeable wrinkles in the fine-grained skin of her forehead. It was, in short, the face of a Kyoto beauty; but it was doll-like as well and quite lacking in expression. Nonetheless, there was no denying that she was beautiful, from the nape of her neck to the tips of her fingers, so beautiful indeed that no one would have taken her for an old woman. It was, moreover, a refined sort of beauty, like that of the dowager of a noble family.

"Such devotion, my dear!" she said, smiling amiably at Komayo. "Your hair is lovely. I suppose you had it done at Sadoya? But then, with such nice hair, any style would be becoming."

"Oh, dear me!" Komayo laughed, as if unsure how to respond. "With the hairpiece, they manage to do it up one way or another."

The clappers were heard from the stage. Segawa urged them to take their time and then abruptly left the room. Tsunakichi followed him into the corridor, carrying a cup of tea with a red lacquer cover. Yamai glanced at Komayo and Hanasuke.

"It would be tragic to miss his debut in the new role," he said, as if delivering a line from a soliloquy, and then he, too, rose to go. Seeing their chance, the women hastily paid their respects to Ohan and hurried out into the corridor. As they retraced their steps through the undercroft, Hanasuke whispered in Komayo's ear.

"Koma-chan, is that lady Segawa-san's mother?"

"Yes, she is."

"She's so beautiful and refined. I thought she must teach flower arranging or the tea ceremony."

"She's always like that—always elegant. Now you see why common girls like us haven't got a chance." Realizing she had raised her voice as she spoke, Komayo looked around, but the dimly lit corridor beneath the stage was deserted, filled only with the sound of hammering from overhead. Apparently, the curtain had not yet opened.

"You see, after everything I've done, it still isn't working. The biggest obstacle is that woman—she doesn't approve, or so he tells me. It makes me utterly miserable."

"It's as if she's already acting like a mother-in-law before you're formally married." For better or worse, Hanasuke always made it a practice to take the part of the person she was talking with; and so even though she knew privately that Segawa was quite fickle and that the mother wasn't solely to blame, she never would have whispered a word of this to Komayo, especially in her current state of excitement when she was so unlikely to have listened. Blurting out disagreeable truths not only hurt other people but also can make one thoroughly disliked, so Hanasuke said only what she thought others wanted to hear. Consequently, Komayo agreed with her completely: as everyone knew, she and Segawa were deeply in love, and if something was preventing their union, she was convinced that it could only be his mother. Worse still, Ohan's friendly, guileless manner made it impossible for her to respond as she would have liked.

"Why doesn't anything in this world go the way we want it to?" Komayo asked, sighing to herself. As they emerged into the theater, the clappers sounded from the stage and the curtain parted. Komayo was immediately caught up in the bright, lively scene in the hall, so different from the dim undercroft, and she hurried off to her seat. Even though he had not been invited, Yamai followed her quietly into the box. No matter where he was, at the theater, at a restaurant, or a teahouse, Yamai would tag along in silence behind any random acquaintance. Seated now between Komayo and Hansuke, he blew clouds of smoke from his Shikishima as he surveyed the scene in the hall and the action on the stage.

17. *Opening Day (II)*

A costume change transformed Jūjirō's radiant figure into an even more splendid sight: a warrior in a suit of scarlet-bound armor. He was as beautiful as the decoration on a New Year's battledore, and all eyes followed him as he made his exit, striking heroic poses along the walkway that ran through the audience. Among those watching were three women seated in a box directly above Komayo's on the east side of the theater. One was a slender woman aged somewhere in her thirties. She wore her hair in the gingko-leaf style, with an imported, antique hair clip decorated with tiny beads of coral. Beneath her sober kimono of silk crepe, a fine-patterned underkimono with a pale blue gray collar of dappled silk was visible. Her *haori* jacket was made of black crepe, and her doubled-faced obi of printed silk was fastened with a clasp made from a plain copper sword hilt, an object that seemed to have a history of its own. She wore only one ring: a diamond of modest size in a platinum setting. Her costume as a whole was discreet but obviously expensive, suggesting that she was a geisha of some seniority. The second woman was perhaps twenty-four or twenty-five. Her hair, done in the lowest of the *marumage* styles offered by the Sadoya, was adorned with a ribbon of mottled lavender silk and a gold lacquer comb dotted with pearls. She wore a conspicuously lavish kimono and *haori* jacket of double-sided Ōshima fabric woven with a pattern of large hexagons. Her obi was a single piece of heavy, embroidered silk held together with a jeweled clasp; and her rings alone—an astonishingly large diamond and another set with a pearl—must have cost at least a thousand yen. Her elaborate toilette, complemented by her long, full face and exceedingly white skin, qualified her as a beauty worthy of attention, and her dress and makeup set her apart from more ordinary women. The third occupant of the box, a woman of about forty, seemed to be the mistress of a *machiai*. But her appearance was vulgar, suggesting that she had come from the provinces and had started life as a maid. As if on cue, the three simultaneously lowered their opera glasses, and their eyes met as they sighed with admiration.

A short time later, at the point that Ichiyama Jūzō, in the role of Takechi Mitsuhide, appeared from behind a gourd trellis, the beautiful girl whose hair was in a *marumage* grasped the hand of the older woman with the gingko-leaf coiffure next to her. "Nee-san, I can't go on like this, admiring him from a distance!" Her voice was quiet but filled with emotion.

"Then you'll just have to invite him to meet you somewhere, won't you?"

"I wish I could! When I was a geisha, I was able to manage that kind of thing, but I feel so awkward now and I never know what to say. And besides, isn't Segawa-san involved with that woman from the Obanaya?"

"You mean Komayo?" said the older woman, her voice full of disdain. "They say she's clever. But don't you think a well-bred girl like you can compete with her?"

"I don't. I might as well give up. What if I were to tell him how I feel and he refused me? That would be worse still." Her tone was so sweet that she seemed almost tongue-tied.

On the stage, the play had now reached the point where the old mother, mortally wounded, was beginning her death soliloquy. Taking advantage of the lull in the action, the two women began to whisper intently to each other. But when Jūjirō, wounded in turn, staggered onto the *hanamichi*, they raised their opera glasses and returned their attention to the stage, as if suddenly waking from a nap. Then again, when Jūjirō had expired and there was nothing left on the stage to hold their gaze, they returned to their whispering.

Because the interlude, "Crossing Lake Biwa," would not be performed for the premiere, when the curtain closed on the tenth act of *Ehon Taikōki*, the performance proceeded directly to the middle piece in the program, *Nijūshikō*. This vignette ended to thunderous applause with Segawa Isshi, in the role of Princess Yaegaki, floating magically above fox fires in the inner garden. Many in the audience felt this was a convenient moment to sneak out for dinner, and the theater restaurant was filled to overflowing. The three women found a table near the entrance and had settled down to watch the parade of customers filing in and out when the younger one suddenly grabbed her companion's sleeve.

"Rikiji-san! There she is."

She looked around to see Komayo and Hanasuke, followed closely by the indefatigable Yamai. Preoccupied perhaps with the task of finding an empty table, Komayo passed quite near without noticing Rikiji, before moving on with her retinue, laughing at some private joke.

Rikiji, a look of frank loathing on her face, laughed derisively in turn as she watched them go.

"Look at that! Who does she think she is? That really is too

much!" She spoke so loudly it would have been difficult not
to overhear.

Rikiji, superior as she was to Komayo in both age and station,
thought it inexcusable of the younger geisha to pass by an elder of
the quarter without any sort of greeting and to laugh as she went.
It made her all the more furious to think that Komayo must have
seen her but had used the crush of the crowd to feign ignorance.
What only made things worse, of course, was that Komaya had
stolen Rikiji's *danna*, Yoshioka-san, some months earlier. Accordingly, she had been determined, if the occasion arose, to have her
revenge, to see Komayo reduced to tears, but there were risks in
confronting her at some engagement and thereby having her own
shame revealed before everyone present. She had hoped for an opportunity at a dance performance or some similar event, but until
today she had waited in vain. Now, at long last, she perhaps saw
her chance in the person of Kimiryū. A geisha who had formerly
been attached to Rikiji's house, Kimiryū had been bought out by a
businessman and set up as his mistress. The man had died recently and had left her the magnificent house in which he had kept her,
the hundred *tsubo* of excellent real estate in the heart of Hama-chō
on which it stood, and ten thousand yen. As a consequence, Kimiryū was now at leisure to decide her future—she might open a
geisha house, or an inn, or a *machiai*, or perhaps a restaurant spe-
cializing in grilled chicken. Or she could leave her precious legacy
untouched and use it as a dowry. She evidently was willing to give
marriage a try if she could find a good-looking man who would
love her and be faithful, one who would always let her have her
way. This last plan certainly seemed to be a safer way of securing a
comfortable future than enduring the hard work and vagaries of a
business. With her own best interests constantly in mind, she had
often come to confer with Rikiji at the Minatoya, and it was this
that had led Rikiji to invite her to the theater today.

During the three years since she left the quarter, Kimiryū devoted herself so completely to her elderly patron that even she
was surprised by her dedication. She never once touched her

shamisen and went only rarely to the theater. In return the old man expressed his affection by making a handsome provision for her in his will. But now that she had fulfilled her duty and been rewarded in kind, she was free in body and spirit. If, as the saying goes, "opportunity makes the thief," then Kimiryū was restless with all the possibilities. Thus coming to the theater tonight after such a long absence, she was overcome at the sight of Segawa Isshi in his debut as Jūjirō and told Rikiji quite clearly that if there were any way to arrange it, she would love to see him after the performance. For a moment, Rikiji recoiled at such a sudden request, but realizing that there could be no more perfect opportunity for revenge on Komayo, in the end she told Kimiryū that she would make an immediate approach on her behalf. Her next step was to go to the Kikyō, one of the teahouses connected with the theater, to talk with the proprietress, a woman she knew well and who was particularly influential in theatrical circles. This resulted in a message sent to Segawa asking if he would come that very evening to the Kutsuwa *machiai* in Tsukiji, even if for only a brief visit.

Thanks to the good offices of the mistress of the Kikyō, who was adept in such matters, the response proved better than they might have hoped, for by the time "Kawashō," the second interlude, was ending, they had a favorable reply, much to the joy of both Kimiryū and Rikiji. As soon as she heard this news, the third member of their party, who was in fact the proprietress of the Kutsuwa, said she would go on ahead to get things ready, and even though the famous "foot-warmer" scene was about to begin, she left the box, giving Kimiryū a hearty slap on the back as she did so. Now that matters had been decided, however, Kimiryū began to lose confidence and fell to brooding. Far from spurring her on, that gesture from the Kutsuwa mistress left her speechless and embarrassed. When the curtain opened to reveal Segawa Isshi, this time in the role of the maiden Koharu, Kimiryū sat behind Rikiji, half covering her face with a handkerchief. Nonetheless, from her hiding place she watched his every move. After a few moments, Rikiji, to her further embarrassment, tugged sharply at her sleeve.

"There!" she said, as if she were beginning an affair herself. "He's looking this way. Kimi-chan, show your face a bit more!"

Kimiryū realized that Segawa was indeed glancing up at their box from time to time as he delivered his lines, but despite Riki-ji's encouragement, she grew even more confused and could only look down at her lap, her face bright red.

18. *Yesterday and Today*

They were in the four-and-a-half mat room at the Gishun that had always been a favorite meeting place for them. Segawa was wearing a double kimono of finely patterned silk, with the crest of his acting family on the back and sleeves, dyed discreetly in reverse colors, as was the practice at the famous house of Daihiko. He sat casually with his legs folded to one side, as a woman would, showing a bit of the material of his underkimono, a yellow brown fabric dyed with a pattern of wheels rolling through waves that could only be a special order from the Erien. His obi, narrow in the old style and tightly bound, was made of satin decorated with a single stripe and marked at one end with the name of the maker embroidered in red. It was most likely the work of the Hiranoya in Hama-chō. On most men, this costume would have been terribly gaudy, but for an *onnagata* it seemed positively inspired. Reaching behind his back with both hands, Segawa pulled the sash still tighter and then sat up more formally on his knees. He took up his pipe case, a lacquered paper tube decorated by Taishin with a design of autumn leaves floating on water, and his tobacco pouch of gilded leather with a fine crimson pattern. The cord that joined them was embellished with a small ball of antique coral, an import no doubt, and the silver clasp on the pouch—of uncertain origin—was in the form of a tiny basket filled with golden pebbles. He thrust them carelessly into his sash.

"O-Koma," he said, calling her by her pet name, "I'm off then. I'll be back in an hour or two, I promise. . . . If you don't have anything to say, at least fetch my *haori*."

Komayo was still wearing her black crepe jacket. She sat by the brazier poking angrily at the ashes with the fire tongs and did not look up as she answered.

"Fine," she said, her tone quite cold. "I'll be waiting." Seizing the flask of saké on the table, she was about to empty it into a teacup that was already close to overflowing when Segawa caught her hand.

"What's the matter with you? Haven't I just explained everything? This isn't like you. I have to meet a visitor from Osaka, someone who has been a supporter of our family since my father's day. Sodezaki-san hasn't been to Tokyo in some time, and he's bringing another admirer with him as well."

"In that case, you must have known about this for some time. But then why did you invite Yamai-san to go out tonight if the performance ended early? I heard you ask him in the dressing room. I would never doubt you if you said you suddenly had an engagement, but this is just too . . ." Plainly furious, Komayo stopped in midsentence, her voice dissolving in tears.

"Fair enough. You simply refuse to understand. If you don't want me to, I just won't go." He spoke sternly in the hope of bullying her, and indeed, even now she couldn't bring herself to tell him not to go but just went on dabbing her eyes with her handkerchief. So then, as if to show that he wasn't in a hurry, he took out the tobacco pouch he'd tucked in his sash and lit his pipe. While he smoked, he went on talking, almost to himself.

"If you tell me not to go, I won't go. It's as simple as that. If Sodezaki-san decides to withdraw his patronage, then so be it." He tapped his pipe on the brazier. "You lost Yoshioka-san because of me, so if I lose someone as well, then we'll be even—no obligations between us, nothing to cause resentment."

At this point, he stretched out on the tatami, as if to say he didn't care what she did. Komayo, weak as she was with love for him, now had no choice but to urge him to go. Segawa, being experienced in the complexities of love affairs, had foreseen this outcome from the beginning. Even if she continued to insist that he stay with her, he was perfectly capable of matching her obstinacy, to the point of shaking her off and walking out the door. He knew quite well that no matter what spiteful things might be said on either side, when it came to moments like this, women were the weaker sex. He did not have to consult the appropriate passages about Yonehachi and Adakichi from *Shunshoku umegoyomi* to know that he could simply let her go for a time and that a kind word from him would eventually bring her to heel. He knew how these things turned out; and besides, the truth was that he had begun to grow a bit weary of Komayo. As soon as he could find a good replacement, he intended to break off his affair with her. Even though things were not actually ending now, he wanted to make sure that their ties did not grow more intimate. It seemed likely that by this time Komayo was deep in debt, and if he were to continue seeing her for another six months or a year, like it or not, he might find himself assuming responsibility as her husband. But if it came to that, he felt sure he'd have the courage to break with her, that in the end she would be no match for him.

For her part, Komayo had been determined to keep him with her tonight at all costs, but it made her uneasy to think how angry he might be later if she insisted on having her way and held him back. After all, she was dealing with Segawa Isshi, a man who, unlike most in his profession, was single-minded, self-indulgent, and incapable of flattery—the very qualities that had made her fall in love with him. Given how hard he'd worked to convince her, perhaps he was telling the truth, perhaps there really was a faithful admirer visiting from Osaka. As she thought it over, her resolve gradually began to weaken.

"It's getting late," she said. "Go quickly and come back just as quickly. I won't make any more trouble." She moved closer to him, stealing a glance at his face.

"What? It doesn't matter if I don't go," he said, sitting up lazily. "I can always apologize later."

"No, I'd be ashamed to make you miss an appointment. It's already past eleven. Please go, and come back as soon as you can. I can't stand waiting by myself, so I'll go to the house for a bit and then come back."

"All right, if you really don't mind, let's meet here later." Segawa made a show of taking her hand, as if he needed help getting up. He rose with apparent reluctance and straightened his collar.

At a moment like this, a woman in love with an actor has to hide her feelings and cheerfully send him off to his engagement, even if it cuts her to the quick to do so. With this unnatural imperative in mind, Komayo stood behind Segawa and helped him into his *haori* as if she were about to embrace him. They might have been actors in some drama from the new theater. Segawa leaned back, pressing his body against Komayo's, and as he reached through the sleeve, he grasped her hand.

"So we're clear, then? Be sure to wait for me."

Without another word, he reached for the door. Carrying the clothing tray with his cape, hat, and scarf in it, Komayo followed him into the hall.

"I'll see you later, then." The proprietress and the maid paid their respects as he climbed into the *rikisha*, and as they passed through the gate of the Gishun, Segawa glanced instinctively at his gold wristwatch. He had known from the start that it would be impossible to keep two engagements on the evening of the opening day, when the performance ended later than usual. But the mistress of the Kikyō had cleverly appealed to the wanton nature common to all men, and now he was restless with impatience, like a small child waiting in agitation for a longed-for toy. He knew he was betraying Komayo, but the Kikyō woman, who seemed very experienced in such matters, had coaxed him along, promising to apologize herself to Komayo later on. "I'll tell her it's all my fault," she'd said, "and that should settle it." So with that invitation, he had taken it on himself to overcome Komayo's reluctance to see him go. Then, too, the full-bodied young woman with the round chignon had seemed something of a beauty when seen from the distance of the stage; and the news that she'd been living much in the manner of a faithful widow, in apparent chastity, since the death of her patron—this further excited his curiosity. In anticipation of what awaited him at his destination, Segawa already had decided that he would not return to the Gishun that night, regardless of the consequences. So, lost in his musings over the delights of this unexpected new romance, he soon found himself pulling up at the gate of the Kutsuwa *machiai* on the far side of the Tsukiji River.

Meanwhile, the mistress of the Gishun invited Komayo to stay with her in the office and pass the time there, even offering to telephone if Segawa were slow in returning. But Komayo, unable to sit quietly and wait, declined the offer, saying she would walk as far as Ginza and then come back later. Without even bothering to call for a *rikisha*, she stepped out of the house into the narrow street lined with *machiai*. It was clogged in both directions with a number of cars and several *rikisha* waiting for customers, and as Komayo set off through them toward the Ministry of Agriculture and Commerce, she hurried as though hoping to avoid being seen.

The early winter night was deep and hazy and so strangely warm that it almost seemed to portend an earthquake. The brilliance of the moon cast sharp shadows in the dry street as if it were still summer. A fresh breeze brushed the hair at her temples. Without really meaning to, Komayo found herself remembering the night when Segawa had first called her to the Gishun. She had parted from him later and walked through the nighttime streets, doubting her own joy, wondering whether it had all been a dream or whether she'd somehow been bewitched. Unwilling to have her precious memories spoiled by the people and cars in the busy streets, she had taken a circuitous path home through dark alleys and byways, even though her knees had been shaking with fatigue.

It was early autumn then, and the days were warmed by the lingering summer heat. In the evening, pleasant autumn winds stirred the sleeves of her kimono, but late at night the cold dew chilled her to the bone. The season was different now, and yet having escaped at last from the long, stifling day at the theater, she found herself once more under a dewy nighttime sky. The light of the moon was clear and brilliant, despite the haze over the house-tops, and the breeze blowing through the darkened streets was soft on her skin. The strains of a shamisen from a strolling player across the river drifted toward her as she glanced up at the lighted window of a *machiai*, visible through a thick hedge—somehow it all reminded her of that unforgettable evening, their first night together, and even as she hurried along, tears welled up in her eyes. Quickly hiding her face with her handkerchief, she looked cautiously around. Fortunately, this side of the street was deep in shadow from the enormous facade of the ministry building. At this hour, the street normally would have been filled with *rikisha* bringing geisha to engagements or coming to retrieve them, the lights of the car companies shining like stars in the night sky: Hiyo-shi, Daisei, Shintake, Mihara, Nakamino, and the others. But this evening, by pure chance, there was nothing to be seen in either direction. A lone car appeared from Uneme Bridge, and then two or three geisha wandered into view, quite drunk, to judge by their loud voices and wild laughter. Looking urgently for a place to hide, Komayo darted to the left at the Kobiki-chō crossing; she wanted a dark alley where she could crouch down and bury her face in the sleeves of her kimono and cry to her heart's content. Nothing else would help. If she could just be alone, with no one to bother her, no one to comfort her, if she could just cry until there were no more tears, then afterward she might feel calmer, might be able to face the world again. She was well acquainted with this solitary side of her nature; and when she found herself at her wit's end, her first impulse was to seek out a hiding place—even a closet would do—where she could have a good cry alone. Afterward she would tell herself that it was a ridiculous habit, but it had begun when she had lived in far-off Akita, where she had spent years with no one able to understand her but her husband. Before she quite realized it, it had become a regular pattern, and she knew very well how difficult it was to break a habit, try as you might. Since that time, it seemed that there had been more things every year that made her want to cry and less leisure to try to break her habit of doing so. Now as she stood weeping in a dark alley, it occurred to her that she had been born to spend her days in tears, a thought that made her sadder still. She cried until the tears could almost have been wrung from her underkimono, the same one she had only just ordered as a matched set with Segawa's.

A car passed, sending up a cloud of dust, and somewhere nearby a dog began to bark. Reluctantly, Komayo left the darkness of the alley and set off again. She had gone only a short way, however, when she came upon two geisha, apparently on their way home from an engagement. She couldn't hear much of the conversation, but she distinctly caught the phrase "master of the Hamamura." They were talking about Segawa Isshi. Instantly, she slipped into the shadows under the eaves, determined to get as close as she could to hear what they were saying. Unaware of her presence, the women prattled on.

"I'm sure it was Segawa-san," said one of them. "I'm green with envy. Where do you suppose they were going?"

"I'll bet you it wasn't. I'll phone Komayo tomorrow and find out without letting on. If it really was him, I'll pay for the next movie."

"And if I'm wrong, I'll pay. But I'm not sure that's a good idea. If it *was* Segawa-san and another geisha, then there's going to be trouble. Komayo might even suspect us. I don't think you should risk phoning her or anyone else."

"I suppose you're right. But who could it be, this other woman?"

Komayo held her breath, waiting to hear the answer, but to no avail. Another car sped by, drowning out the rest of the conversation. In the meantime, the two geisha had reached the lattice door of a *machiai*, and Komayo could hear them greeting the mistress of the house as they disappeared inside. By now she was beside herself. She hadn't heard much, but she'd heard enough to know that she could no longer stand idly by and wait: she would have to phone the Kutsuwa, where Segawa had said he was going, to see whether or not he was there. If it proved to be an innocent engagement, it would hardly matter if someone recognized her voice. Wondering why she hadn't thought of this solution before, she almost broke into a run as she turned and headed back the way she'd come. Arriving at the Gishun, she hurried into the office and snatched up the phone.

When she spoke, however, she was careful to sound calm and composed. "Is that the Kutsuwa? Would you be so kind as to call Segawa-san to the phone? . . . Who is this? I . . . I'm calling from the Segawa residence."

She waited for a few minutes, without hearing anything more. In a fit of rage, she screamed into the receiver to call the woman back, but just at that moment the lines were crossed and the connection was broken. The maid, O-Maki, had been standing nearby. Unwilling to see Komayo in such a state, she took the phone from her and called again. "He should be getting home at any moment," she was told. Since Komayo had already said she was calling from Segawa's house, she could hardly go on protesting now. Despite her disappointment, it occurred to Komayo that he might have told them he was going home even as he was heading back to join her at the Gishun, and so she settled down to wait. But by the time the clock struck twelve, she again was in a frenzy. This time she called the Kutsuwa and left her name. "Tell him it's Komayo, that she's expecting him at the Gishun." After being kept waiting longer than was polite, she was told again that he'd gone back to his house in Tsukiji. Half-mad by now, she called Segawa's home, only to be put off with a simple "He's not in."

At this point it was clear that no one knew where to find him.

But it was midnight, the hour when the gates of the *machiai* had to be closed. Out of kindness to Komayo, O-Maki shut only one side of the gate. "He's bound to be back soon," she said, her voice louder than necessary. As she stood in the street, a short man in a suit suddenly appeared and staggered drunkenly toward her. Startled, O-Maki was about to close the gate when the man called out.

"Hey! Wait a minute! It's me. Is Komayo-san here?"

"Oh!" O-Maki laughed. "I'm sorry, I didn't recognize you. . . . You were here last night."

"Yes, that's it. It's Yamai," he said, and before he had finished speaking, before the maid had a chance to turn him away, his shoes were off and he had shown himself in. It was a skill learned from long experience.

19. *Yasuna*

Two or three days later, an item, fully a column and a half in length, appeared in the *Miyako* gossip sheet under the title "Komayo Distraught."

Last autumn we were treated to *Yasuna* at the Kabukiza, and this spring we had *The River Sumida*, both triumphs, both portrayals of madness, which ensured that no one in the Shimbashi quarter could fail to have heard the name of the dancer, Komayo, the celebrated geisha of the Obanaya. But now, on the opening night of the new season at the Shintomiza, her very dear friend, the actor Segawa Isshi of the Hamamuraya, has been stolen away from her, and try as she might to sleep, she lies awake waiting for him until dawn. If she were less than human—were just a pretty figurine—she might have felt no jealousy and remained calm and quiet. But instead, on the night in question, the madness in her was real enough, and she was seen trampling on her dancing fan.

The writer had parodied a passage in the *Yasuna* ballad, creating elaborate puns between Segawa's name and a celebrated kabuki play. Still, this alone wasn't so damaging, since it was only an unsubstantiated newspaper article. No one took these things very seriously in the floating world of actors and geisha, and such rumors were generally forgotten almost as soon as they began to circulate. But surprisingly, this was an exception. At the bath, at the hairdresser's, in the waiting rooms of teahouses, in the rehearsal rooms of the music and dance teachers—in short, just about anywhere geisha tend to gather—the rumor continued to grow, day after day, giving rise to even newer rumors. Thus not one of the Shimbashi geisha who crowded the Shintomiza failed to take a good look at Kimiryū. The run, which had been filling the house for each performance, was nearing its midpoint, but it still was common to hear whispered confirmations of another sighting. Indeed, from the opening day, Kimiryū was in constant attendance. If she was not in her box, she could be found in the corridors; if not in the dressing rooms, then in the theater teahouses or the dining room. She could always be spotted somewhere. What's more, on the fourth or fifth day a splendid curtain appeared, lowered and raised just for the middle piece, *Nijūshikō*, and on it were embroidered inscriptions indicating that it had been offered to the master of the Hamamura by five geisha from the Minatoya, with Rikiji's name listed first. In the midst of all this, someone began spreading a new rumor that next year, on the occasion of his succession to his father's professional name, Segawa Isshi, head of the Hamamuraya, would take Kimiryū as his wife. Soon someone claimed to have seen the betrothal gifts exchanged by the couple, and someone else insisted that the two had actually been engaged long ago when Kimiryū was still a geisha.

This last rumor sounded quite plausible. In fact, some people had found the overnight change from talk of an affair to stories about a wedding to be unreasonably quick, but now even they were persuaded that there was something to it.

When word finally reached Komayo, she resigned herself to her ruin. For his part, Segawa seized on the rumors as the most convenient excuse for his actions. As a result, they never even discussed whether or not they were true. Convinced that they were, Komayo was driven to the verge of a breakdown and wailed at his disloyalty. But Segawa, weary of the tears and reproaches whenever they met and at a loss for further excuses which she would reject in any case, chose to disappear. By contrast, Kimiryū had all the liveliness and spirit of a new lover and no reason to say anything unpleasant. So the more difficult things became with Komayo, the more deeply involved Segawa became with Kimiryū.

One day, when they found themselves at the Kutsuwa, Segawa spoke to Kimiryū about the rumors.

"There's been a lot of talk about the two of us getting married. As soon as names get linked, it always comes to that."

"It must be hard for you."

"No, I was thinking how much trouble it could cause you. I'm very sorry."

"But why should it bother me? I'm not sure I understand what you mean."

"With all these rumors, it must be hard for you to go out, at least for the moment."

"That's why I said it must be difficult for you. Besides, you had Komayo-san, and then I came along. I don't know how you could forgive me if I caused problems between the two of you."

"I'd prefer that you not mention her name. . . . But there's another interesting story making the rounds. They're saying that we've been engaged ever since the days when you were at Rikiji's house. Then we were separated for a time when your patron bought your contract. It's partly Rikiji's fault—apparently a geisha asked her whether or not the story was true, and she insisted it was. In fact, I got so tired of the questions myself that I said it was, too. I even told a certain geisha, who shall remain nameless, the same thing."

"And what did she do then?"

"What did she do? I don't know because I haven't seen her since."

"It's funny—I feel as though I really have known you a long time, not just a few days. Why have things turned out this way?"

"What do you mean?"

"Nii-san, promise me you won't ever leave me." With that, Kimiryū burst into tears for no apparent reason, as women are in the habit of doing.

Having accepted the invitation to see her, Segawa spent the night at the house in Hama-chō where she'd been kept as a mistress. That first night led to a second and then a third, and finally he began commuting each day from her house to the theater. Soon his servant, Tsunakichi, and his *rikisha* man, Kumako, took up residence there as well. Naturally enough, the managers and anyone else at the theater who had urgent business with Segawa began to call on him in Hama-chō, and his house in Tsukiji came to be regarded as a place for occasional visits only. Even though no plaque had been hung by the gate announcing his presence, the house in Hama-chō had, in effect, become his main residence. And Kimiryū, her hair always done now in the *marumage* style of a married woman, was effectively his wife.

In the wake of these developments, Segawa's adoptive mother, Ohan, no doubt pleased at the prospect of Kimiryū's considerable fortune, went to the trouble of paying a call at the Hama-chō house and asking her to continue to favor her son. Then when Kimiryū returned the call, she was received so warmly that she decided she could love Ohan as she loved her own mother. Soon, the two of them became fast friends and began going to the theater together, not only to the Shintomiza, but also to the Imperial, the Ichimuraza, and a number of others.

Meanwhile, in one Shimbashi teahouse after another, among the geisha and the actors and entertainers of her acquaintance, Rikiji of the Minatoya was tirelessly but subtly spreading favorable rumors about Kimiryū, stories designed to paint her in the most sympathetic of lights.

20. *The Morning Bath*

It was eleven o'clock in the morning, the hour when the Hiyoshi public bath was nearly deserted. In fact, there was only one bather in the large tub—old Gozan, master of the Obanaya, who was enjoying not only the warmth but also the luxury of solitude. Loudly yawning, he stretched his thin, bony arms until it seemed they might come out of their sockets and then sat back to admire the way the bright winter sunlight fell at an angle from the window in the high ceiling, sparkling in the clean, hot water. At that moment, the glass door at the entrance clattered open to reveal a man of about forty. He was dark skinned, with a thick, powerful neck and wide shoulders ill suited to his padded silk kimono. His collar was noticeably soiled, but he wore his clothes with a certain style. His sash was of soft silk crepe, starched only in front. He wore no jacket, but his moustache had been carefully trimmed. No one would have taken him for a journalist or a lawyer; in fact, it was hard to believe he practiced any honest profession. As he was taking off his kimono, he studied the theater and variety hall posters on the wall of the dressing room, but his look was hard, almost a scowl. Rattling open the door between the dressing room and the bath, he strode over to the tub and began splashing himself. At this point, having warmed himself for long enough, Gozan stood up; and the newcomer, catching sight of him, grunted a simple greeting, much as a student might. He was about to plunge into the tub but stopped himself, apparently finding it a bit too hot.

"There's nothing like a public bath, is there, Takaraya-san?" Gozan said to him with a hint of irony in his voice. "A tub at home is convenient, but it doesn't make you want to hum a tune." As he spoke, Gozan sensed another yawn coming on but suppressed it. He felt no particular animosity toward the master of the Takaraya, but there was something about him he disliked. It was said that he'd been in the service of a troupe of itinerant actors before starting the Takaraya. It was a disreputable establishment, and until just four or five years ago, the mere mention of the name would draw knowing looks from Shimbashi customers and geisha alike—"Oh, *that* house." But precisely because of the sort of business it did, the Takaraya soon prospered; and after suddenly taking on two or three accomplished geisha and sprinkling liberal tips among the important teahouses, the master quickly reopened a more respectable house. Then last year, when there were difficulties in the geisha association and new committee members were chosen, he mounted a successful campaign and began to wield considerable influence. Gozan realized that the master of the Takaraya was another of the nouveaux riches—as the newspapers liked to call them—who were rising from the ranks, and the thought depressed him. In the beginning, the man cared nothing for appearances and resorted to all kinds of sordid expedients; but once he made some money, he used it to gain every possible advantage, forgetting where he had come from and putting on airs. To Gozan, such behavior might be permissible in a politician, a businessman, or a stockbroker, but the master of a geisha house generally should be a dilettante whose refined tastes were an obstacle to any chance of material success and who ran his house as a kind of hobby. Every aspect of such an establishment should be cultivated and elegant. Such was Gozan's thinking in his youth, and he saw no reason to change it now. But when he saw the master of the Taka-raya, everything seemed wrong. First, there was his moustache, which was not at all to Gozan's liking. Then there was his manner since he'd been elected to the committee: during discussions of the association's finances or other such matters, any competing comment was liable to touch off a harangue from him, as though he were giving a speech to the shareholders' meeting of a corporation. It was utterly ludicrous.

But the man seemed oblivious to the hatred he aroused. If not, then perhaps he was determined to take advantage of his audacity and cunning, qualities he believed to be the keys to success. In any event, he seemed unconcerned at the old man's ambiguous answer and his half-suppressed yawn.

"Sensei, is it true you've retired from the variety halls after that little incident?" He had climbed into the bathtub now.

"At my age, I couldn't perform even if I wanted to." Gozan was seated on the draining platform, scrubbing his sides, his ribs visible under the skin. "If I did go back, I'd only cause trouble—for the theater owners and spectators alike."

"But they don't seem to have anything worthwhile to offer these days, which is probably why the halls often are empty. By the way, I've been meaning to call on you to discuss a little matter, but as you can imagine, I've been busy." He looked casually around the men's bath, but they still were the only customers, and there was no sound from the women's bath. The only other person in sight was the bespectacled old woman seated at the elevated reception desk, but she was absorbed in ripping the seams from some ancient garment.

"Actually, we'd like to ask if you'd be willing to become a member of the committee. Since you're no longer performing, you should have the time, and we'd be very grateful if we could count on your help. . . ." He was quickly lapsing into his oratorical style. In order to expand his influence on the committee, Taka-raya had forced the departure of the older members one after the other, replacing them with mediocrities who had little influence.

The idea behind it was ultimately to arrange everything to his own advantage. As the master of the Obanaya, one of the oldest and most respected houses in Shimbashi, Gozan was known throughout the district as a stubborn, difficult old man, but the locals knew that he was also a good man, one who was extremely frank and hadn't the slightest trace of greed in him. It was this reputation that had given Takaraya the idea of trying to persuade him to join the committee. Since the old man was known to dislike wasting his breath on trivial matters, he could be expected to hold his peace at meetings, which made him a far better choice than someone who might prove to be a threat of some sort. But perhaps Gozan had guessed what was in his mind, for his answer was curt.

"No, you'll have to excuse me. My wife hasn't been well lately, and I'm too old myself. I'd be no use at all."

"I'm sorry to hear you say so. You're an important man in the quarter and a respected one."

At this point, they were interrupted by the bath attendant. "It's got quite cold, hasn't it?" he said, coming in to wash Takaraya's back. Then three more customers appeared in quick succession. The first, a pale man of about thirty wearing gold-rimmed glasses, was the husband of a well-known hairdresser, O-Kō, who was reputed in the quarter to be a very wealthy woman. He had once been a narrator for silent films, but now he was little more than her dependent. The second—fat, bald, and about fifty—was the proprietor of the Ichijū, a restaurant that specialized in yakitori. He was accompanied by a sickly boy of twelve or thirteen who had a crippled leg—what was commonly called a "duck's leg." They all lived nearby and knew one another, so they exchanged greetings as they entered the bath. They divided up naturally, Gozan and the master of the Ichijū on the one hand and Takaraya and the husband of the hairdresser on the other, with the latter pair launching into a discussion about the geisha in various quarters. After a few moments, Takaraya seemed to remember something.

"Actually, we've had a geisha of that sort lately even in Shimbashi, and some of our committee members are complaining privately that it could hurt the reputation of the quarter."

"Really? Who is she?"

"You haven't heard of her? She's called Ranka."

"What house is she from?"

"It's less than a month since her debut, but there's hardly anyone in Shimbashi who doesn't know about her."

"Is that so?" said the hairdresser's husband. His interest apparently piqued, he didn't even bother to wash the soap from his eyes. "She sounds fascinating. What sort of woman is she? Is she pretty?"

"Don't get excited. If I sing her praises, I'll have O-Kō-san angry with me later."

"But that only makes me more curious!"

The master of the Takaraya laughed. "In my view, she's not really a geisha at all, but she's certainly as amazing in the flesh as she is to hear about. Rumors have a way of spreading—you can't go anywhere or meet anyone nowadays without hearing about Ranka—but ever since she developed this reputation, she's been incredibly popular. She's a character, and quite clever."

"But what does she do that's so unusual? Does she dance in the nude?"

"Yes, she does, actually, but it isn't anything vulgar like 'The Drizzling Rain.' I've heard about it only from the girls at my house, so I'm not sure, but it seems she doesn't really dance at all—she just appears nude at banquets. They say this sort of thing is quite popular at variety halls in the West these days. Apparently, she announces the name of some famous statue and then strikes the pose—wearing snow white tights and a white wig to make herself look like marble. That's why it hasn't been easy to lodge a complaint against her. At any rate, she's one of those 'New Women,' and if you did object, you'd never hear the end of it. Some of the things she says at her engagements are quite wild—for example, that the trouble every year over nude paintings at the Education Ministry exhibition comes from the fact that Japanese people don't understand the beauty of the naked body. This she finds deplorable, so she gives her own little exhibitions for the 'aesthetic education of gentlemen of quality.'"

"Amazing! I think I might need a bit of aesthetic education myself."

"But she doesn't show up for just any party. They say she has three or four engagements every night. It's absurd, isn't it?"

As the two men went on with their ribald conversation, the talk between the master of the Ichijū and Gozan was quite different: theirs was the endless grumbling of old men, a catalog of misfortunes.

"This boy is twelve this year, but what can I do with him in this state? I've decided to forget about school for him." Ichijū was scrubbing his son's pale, emaciated back. "I suppose it's my punishment for killing all those chickens. I'm serious—it's not a joking matter."

The boy's crippled leg was not his only problem; his whole body seemed to be poorly developed, and his mental capacity appeared to be lacking as well. His expression was blank, and he neither spoke nor showed any sign of normal playfulness. He merely sat staring vacantly at nothing in particular. Gozan studied father and son with a look of genuine pity.

"People have always said things like that, but if it were true, then all the boys at the fish market would be cripples, too. They even say you shouldn't go into the eel business, that eels are living creatures just like fish and that killing them brings bad luck, deformity, and disease. But that sort of disease is all in your head. Besides, look at me, I've got a son of my own who makes me want to weep."

"Takijirō, isn't it? What's happened to him?"

"It's not easy to talk about. Three years ago, I heard a rumor that he was staying at a saké bar near Asakusa Park. I'd already given up any hope for him once before, but I thought I'd go anyway and make some inquiries and then perhaps try to reason with him if I could. You know the feelings a father has for his own flesh and blood. So I went around gathering information at the bars in the neighborhood."

"Of course. Just as any parent would."

"But when I heard what people were saying about him, I was stunned. They said he'd sold his soul to the devil. Even if I could find him and tell him what I thought of him, it would only make things worse. I decided that he was a lost cause and went straight home, and I've never said a word about it since, not even to Jūkichi."

"But what did you find out?"

"It hardly bears repeating. He lives with a woman—I suppose she's practically his wife—and he seems to think nothing of it when she brings in customers. They say he even sends her out to his own friends and acquaintances and uses her in appalling movies, the kind you have to hide from the police. And to top it all off, he gambles away the proceeds. No one in the neighborhood has a good thing to say about him, even the prostitutes who are in the same business, and they all sympathize with the woman. When someone is so completely rotten, there's really nothing to be done. At any rate, when I heard all this, I decided to break with him once and for all; but it still bothers me to think he'll eventually cause problems with the authorities. I sometimes wonder whether this is my punishment for making a living for so many years by telling stories about gamblers and gambling."

Just at that moment, the outer glass door clattered open and a woman who looked like a maid hurried into the entrance hall.

"Master!" she called out, panting for air.

"What is it?" said the old man. "What's the matter?"

"It's the mistress!"

"What's wrong? Is she ill? Then come and help me dry off."

21. *Turmoil*

In the spring of that year, Jūkichi, the mistress of the Obanaya, had had a mild stroke and had collapsed during an engagement at a teahouse. Since then, she'd given up her beloved saké and had tried to smoke as little as possible. Today, with an appointment booked for two o'clock, she'd gone early to the hairdresser's, and it was just as she was arriving home that she had the attack, right next to the telephone. She now was completely unconscious, with a loud snore the only sign of life.

O-Sada, the attendant, was out making the rounds of the teahouses and *machiai* to collect bills; the two apprentices were at their lessons; and Hanasuke had just gone off to visit the local shrine. So only the maid, O-Shige, and Komayo were left in the house. It was the last day of the performance at the Shintomiza, and Komayo, thinking it was time she went for a bath, was just taking her combs from her dressing stand. Suddenly the maid called out for help, and Komayo ran down the stairs to find Jūkichi collapsed on the floor. Although O-Shige panicked, Komayo sent her running off to the bath to find Gozan and then phoned for a doctor. She wanted to move Jūkichi to the sitting room, but she was unable to do so alone. So she brought a quilt from the back room and was just about to wrap her in it when Gozan and O-Shige came hurrying back, all out of breath. Together, the three of them managed to get Jūkichi into the back room for the time being. The doctor arrived soon afterward and examined the patient, but he said he couldn't offer a prognosis until he saw how she passed the night. At any rate, for the moment it would be better not to try to move her to a hospital. There was nothing to be done but let her rest quietly. Having given his instructions to Gozan, the doctor left. A nurse was to come shortly, and soon the members of the household who had been absent began arriving, one after another. Somehow they organized themselves to help look after Jūkichi, but they hardly had a chance to catch their breath when a long parade of well-wishers began arriving, spurred on by the rumors flying through the quarter: geisha, of course, but also the proprietors of various houses, *machiai* mistresses, professional jesters, attendants, and numerous others—all coming to express their sympathy. The lattice door never stopped sliding open and shut, and the telephone rang off the hook. The confusion would have made even a healthy person ill. The attendant was too busy with the telephone to find time to eat; and Komayo and Hana-suke, welcoming visitors at the entrance, never even had time for a cigarette. At some point, however, when the lights in the house first went on, the flow of visitors finally began to abate.

"Koma-chan, let's order something to eat while we have a moment. What would you like?"

"I suppose we should. I haven't eaten anything since this morning. But somehow I haven't got much appetite."

"Let's get some foreign food, it's simpler." Hanasuke was getting up to go to the phone when it began ringing. She answered it and responded to a question, then "Just a moment, please—Koma-chan, it's the mistress of the Gishun. She's calling from the Shintomiza."

Komayo took the phone. "Oh really? I do apologize, but we're in a bit of a crisis here—you see, the mistress has fallen ill, and I didn't even have time to phone you. I'm really very sorry." The conversation continued for a few minutes in hushed tones, and then Komayo hung up.

"Koma-chan, it's the last day at the Shintomi, isn't it? I'd completely forgotten. Shouldn't you be going?"

"I've just refused. I can't go out today, no matter what."

"But why? This isn't a private house; if you have an engagement, you go—that's our business. You should at least put in an appearance. I'm free this evening, so I can look after anyone who comes. It's fine, really. The mistress seems to be resting more comfortably, so you should go now and show your face."

"But I haven't even had a bath yet today, and look at my hair." As if intent on ruining it, Komayo tugged roughly at her chignon, which was in fact still quite tidy. She shook her head irritably. "If things were the way they used to be, I'd be going no matter what, but now that he's made his decision, there's no point. If I did go, I'd just see things I'd rather not see and hear things that would make me miserable. No, it's better if I don't go out at all."

"But that's where you're wrong. It's because you're giving in that he's been so full of himself and does just as he pleases. If I were you, I'd scratch his eyes out, and I wouldn't care who was there to see me do it."

"But what good would that do—now that he's in love with someone else? You see, I've learned my lesson." Komayo's tone suggested she'd made up her mind. "Hana-chan, if he's finally decided, then I can't show my face. I'm going to have to leave the quarter."

"The trouble with you is that you always take such a gloomy view. Men are all the same when it comes to a new affair. They get completely carried away for a time. But you know the old saying: 'The trunk is always better than the branches'—in other words, there's no love like the first love. If you're patient, you'll win out in the end. So stop making excuses and go show your face. You know I would never give you bad advice."

Komayo had made it sound as though she were unwilling to go to the engagement, but the truth was that she would never be satisfied if she didn't go. So now, having held herself back so long, she found that Hanasuke's encouragement made her all the more anxious to be off.

"Well, then perhaps I will go for just a little while. I suppose Jūkichi-san will be all right, won't she?"

"If something happens, I'll phone you right away."

"Hana-chan, I don't know how to thank you."

After stopping in the kitchen to get some hot water to smooth her hair, Komayo quietly climbed the stairs to the second floor and knelt in front of her mirror. On any other day, the room would have been almost unbearably noisy, but today it was empty and sad. A bright light had been left on, and—perhaps it was her imagination—the sight of its reflection in the mirror seemed somehow eerie. Under normal circumstances, she would have had the attendant to help her dress, but now she took the kimono from the chest and began her own preparations. She found it awkward to tie the obi and make the final adjustments by herself, but she hurried to finish dressing, as if eager to flee the solitude of the upper floor of the house. As she turned to go, a long, slender object fell at her feet. Startled, she took a step back, but looking more closely she realized it was her obi clasp, the copper-colored one engraved with a spinning wheel.

She remembered how one day, quite early in their affair, the two of them had left the Gishun and wandered through the city. As they were approaching Komayo's street, in Takekawa-chō, they passed the Hamamatsu accessory shop. Without warning, Segawa had opened the door and led her inside. They were shown various rare and elegant objects, bags and accessories of all sorts, but Komayo's eye had fallen on a clasp embellished with a spinning wheel. Taken by the pun between the character for a wheel and one in Segawa's name, she had bought it on the spot, while he had found one decorated with a colt, echoing the first character in Komayo's name. Segawa's family had been regular customers at the Hamamatsuya for generations, and it was said that no actor from any of the great families—the Narita, Otawa, Takashima or Tachibana—would carry accessories that weren't furnished by the store.

Komayo retrieved the precious clasp and was about to fasten it to her obi when she noticed that the pin had somehow come unsprung. As soon as she closed it, it fell open again. This little annoyance, minor though it was, somehow left her feeling quite forlorn and discouraged. Still, having no choice, she found an old pearl clasp she'd had for some time and put it on instead. Then she crept downstairs and fled the house.

When she arrived at the theater a short time later, Komayo knew immediately that there had never been a day as awkward or hateful as this one—and that the trouble with the clasp had been an undeniable sign. Since the performance had started long ago, there was no teahouse attendant to show her to her box, so she stood waiting quietly until a maid she recognized came hurrying down the stairs. But when Komayo asked to be taken to her seat, she was told that the mistress of the Gishun had left the box and that she'd said no one else would be coming. Thus it had already been given to other customers. The teahouse proprietor now appeared and apologized profusely, and at last they managed to find another seat for her and led her to it. But it turned out to be badly situated, in a position that was far too visible, and she felt miserable sitting there alone. Escaping into the hall, she found a spot near an entrance where she could peek in at the audience, but the first thing she saw was the face of her rival, Kimiryū, seated in a center box over on the east side. Her great *marumage* coiffure was decorated with a red ribbon, and around her sat Rikiji of the Minatoya, the mistress of the Kutsuwa, and even Segawa's stepmother, Ohan, with whom she seemed to be having an intimate chat. The thought that Kimiryū had succeeded in winning over Ohan to such a degree filled Komayo with an indescribable sadness. To her eyes, it seemed that Kimiryū already was like a bride who was getting along well with her new mother-in-law, and the realization that this had all come about without her knowledge made Komayo feel as though she'd been cast out, like a total stranger. She already was past grief and anger and even tears, but realizing that it would be too mortifying to be seen by so many people who knew her, she left the theater in a daze without even knowing what play was in progress on the stage. Hurrying home, she went straight upstairs and threw herself down in front of her mirror.

22. *One Thing or Another*

On the third day after her collapse, toward dawn, Jūkichi of the Obanaya went at last to join her ancestors. Her ashes were interred at the family temple in Yotsuya Samegahashi, and in due course the seventh-day service was held. By the time the customary gift of bean-jam cakes wrapped in a crepe kerchief had been distributed to those who had helped defray the costs of the funeral and all the other details had been seen to, the end of the year was at hand. Fortunately, the attendant knew all about the day-to-day running of the house; but now that Jūkichi was gone, old Gozan had no idea what to do about such matters as choosing the New Year's kimono for the geisha and apprentices. At a gathering of his closest friends on the night of the service, he'd already given a hint about his intentions. Since it was out of the question for a man to continue to run the house alone, he would sell it or turn it over to someone who wanted to continue the business. He could then rent a second-floor room somewhere and resume his career as a storyteller. This was how he would pass the years left to him, few though they might be.

The attendant, O-Sada, had hardly slept the night before, busy as she was with preparing the year-end gifts for the teahouses frequented by the Obanaya geisha. Then this morning, she had made the rounds, distributing them to the most important houses. On her return, she found old Gozan occupied, as was his custom, with papers and documents he had taken from the chests and storage boxes. Looking up, he noticed that she had sweat beading her forehead despite the chilliness of the season.

"I appreciate everything you've done," he said. Before continuing, he took off his glasses—the kind old men wear, in heavy brass frames. "You should probably have a rest. I don't know what I'd do if you wore yourself out and got sick. By the way, O-Sada, when you have a moment, would you come in here? There still are a number of things I want to ask you about."

"What sorts of things?"

"Actually, it's about the girls upstairs. They must understand the situation. I haven't said anything to them yet, but perhaps you can tell me what they're thinking."

"Well, it seems that Hanasuke-san is considering moving to another house if you say she should."

"I see. It's lucky that Kikuchiyo was bought off last year. That leaves only Hanasuke and Komayo. The other two are still apprentices, so they should be no problem."

"I think Komayo-san said she wants to go away, somewhere in the country."

"What? Leave Tokyo? Has she lost her mind? Just between you and me, I've been thinking that when she marries Segawa and goes off to the Hamamuraya, I would cancel her debt to mark the occasion."

"Oh, *danna*, I'm afraid things aren't going to work out so nicely. That's been over for some time now."

"Really? They've broken it off? I'd been hoping I could help them, in my own small way. Is it really over?"

"I don't know the details, but it seems there's no chance of his marrying her."

"Is that so? It's awful to grow old—you lose track of things, people's feelings for each other."

"They say that Segawa-san is going to marry Kimiryū, the one who used to be at the Minatoya, early next spring. Everyone's talking about it."

"I see now. That's why Komayo thinks she can't stay here and wants to run off to the country. Poor thing! But isn't she giving up too quickly? Shouldn't she stick up for herself more?"

"I'm not sure, but Hanasuke-san said that she made quite a fuss for a while—so much so that everyone was worried. I have to admit I was concerned myself, but then the mistress fell ill and there was the funeral, and that seemed to distract her. And now she seems to be more or less resigned to the whole thing."

"This other woman, is she a beauty?"

"Kimiryū-san? I knew her some time ago—she wasn't particularly good looking. She's tall and well built, the kind that attracts attention. But they say it isn't her looks, it's her fortune that made Segawa-san change his mind."

"So he was blinded by her money. If that's the kind of man he is, Komayo's well rid of him. But she must be miserable. I feel sorry for the poor girl."

"I think it would cheer her up to hear you say that." At that moment the telephone rang, and O-Sada went to answer it. As she closed the door behind her, the room was left in shadow. Even though Gozan had just finished his lunch, the days had grown shorter with the approach of the solstice. In the gloom, the gilding on the new mortuary tablet seemed to catch the light of the candles burning on the household altar. Rubbing his hips, Gozan stood up to turn on the light. He paused a moment to hold a match to the incense that had gone out on the altar and then turned back to the job of going through the drawers.

"Komayo's contract," he muttered to himself, studying the extract from her family register that was attached to the document. Her name, Masaki Koma, and her birth date were written in the register, along with a note that her parents were deceased. "Both gone," Gozan murmured.

Komayo lost her mother at about the time she started elementary school, and the woman who replaced her was so cruel that the girl's grandmother took her back to her mother's home to raise her. Her father, who was a plasterer, died in the meantime, and her old grandmother also passed away while Komayo was with her husband in Akita—so she was completely alone in the world.

Up until now, Gozan had left the management of the geisha house to Jūkichi. He'd been consulted on the occasional problem, but in general he felt that a man shouldn't meddle in women's business. Women should settle their affairs themselves, he'd said, and he had avoided getting involved. So today, for the very first time, he was seeing the terms of her bond, and for the first time he fully understood how lonely her life had been. When Gozan realized that his wife was going to die, he thought of Taki-jirō, the son who fled their house. He'd wanted to bring him home while his mother was still alive, so she could have one last look at him, even if she were beyond speaking. Swallowing his pride, he had told his tale to a man at the geisha registration office and asked his help in finding the boy. Through him, Gozan learned that since last spring, the police had been cracking down on prostitution in Asakusarokku and that Takijirō, finding business disappointing, had gone off to Kobe without leaving an address. At this news, even stouthearted, stubborn old Gozan was struck by the frailty and emptiness of old age. Now discovering by chance how things stood with Komayo—that she, too, was on her own, with no one to depend on—he couldn't help but feel a deep sympathy for her.

Night was falling. Outside, the electric wires whispered in the winter wind and the bells of the passing *rikisha* rang with a piercing sound that marked the month as December. The geisha and apprentices had gone off to their engagements, and Komayo, who had complained of not feeling well, was left alone upstairs. Taking advantage of this opportunity, Gozan called her down to join him in the sitting room.

"What's wrong?" he asked her. "Have you caught a cold?"

"It's nothing, really, but my nose is sore." Her voice was nasal, and she looked pale as she sat staring at her lap. Gozan noticed how the shadow of her low *shimada* hairdo, even down to the locks that had come loose at the back, showed on the sliding door beneath the altar, and it struck him as somehow very sad.

"They say that sickness is all in the mind, that you just have to cheer up. . . . But there was something else I wanted to talk to you about. I hear you want to go away to the country. I know it's none of my business, but I think you should think careful-ly before you do anything rash. You see, I know all about your situation, all about the master of the Hamamuraya. And I understand why you want to go somewhere else to work, why you feel you can't bear to stay here now that your fiancé has been taken away from you. But that's what I want to discuss. If there were a way for you to save face, am I right to assume you wouldn't want to leave?"

Komayo nodded without looking up. Gozan had unconsciously lapsed into his stage voice, adopting the tone he used to narrate a melodrama.

"As it happens, I was just reading the terms of your bond for the first time, and I see that you're all on your own, with no parents, no brothers or sisters. But if you insist, as a point of pride, on going off somewhere where you don't know a single soul, you'll end up feeling miserable, and nothing good will come of it. Why don't you stay here instead and put up with the unpleasantness for a while? I'm sure you've already realized that I won't be able to run the house alone now that Jūkichi is gone. Even if I could find my son, he's still a man and we'd be no better off. So I've decided to turn over my interest in the house to somebody else if I can find the right person. I don't really need the income now to get by—I can always go off somewhere and earn my living with my tongue. So what do you say? Would you like to have a try at being the mistress of the Obanaya? Wouldn't you like to show everyone in the quarter what you're capable of? What do you think?"

Komayo was too surprised by this proposal to make any reply, and hearing no objection, Gozan, with the impatience of the elderly, had already decided the matter by himself.

"Having an old man around a geisha house spoils the atmosphere, so I'll find a place somewhere nearby. . . . But Komayo, you should know that I own the house itself—I had it rebuilt ten years ago—but the lot, about thirty-three square meters, is rented for five yen a year. You can pay me whatever you can afford for the rent of the house and the use of the name. I'll speak with Hanasuke and the other geisha and with the attendant. If they don't like the idea, we can arrange for them to go elsewhere. Then you could start over with new girls and run the business as you like. It will put my mind at ease to have you take over. Then one day, when you've worked hard and made your fortune, you can pay me what you see fit for the right to the Obanaya name. Well, do we have a deal?"

"Oh *danna*! This is all too wonderful. I don't know what to say."

"Which is why I've arranged the whole thing. In any case, it will be a great relief to have everything decided. . . . Komayo, would you mind phoning for the masseuse to come in a little while? I'm going for a bath."

With that, he went off, old towel in hand, without even turning to see her look of astonishment. After she had made the call, she added some coals to the brazier and settled quietly in front of the household altar. But suddenly she was overcome, with either joy or sorrow, and for a time she hid her face in the sleeves of her kimono.